Paul Blake

Expelled

A Story of Eascote School

Paul Blake

Expelled
A Story of Eascote School

ISBN/EAN: 9783743400399

Manufactured in Europe, USA, Canada, Australia, Japa

Cover: Foto ©Andreas Hilbeck / pixelio.de

Manufactured and distributed by brebook publishing software
(www.brebook.com)

Paul Blake

Expelled

EXPELLED:

A Story of Eastcote School.

BY

PAUL BLAKE.

LONDON AND NEW YORK:
FREDERICK WARNE AND CO.
1886.

Morrison & Gibb, Edinburgh.
Printers to Her Majesty's Stationery Office.

PREFACE.

——o——

I HAD some thoughts of dedicating the following pages to boys who had been expelled from school. But on reflection it was evident that they were the very boys who would not care to read a book touching on such a subject. Then, too, an old proverb occurred to me about locking the door after the steed was stolen.

So I resolved, on the principle that prevention is better than cure, to dedicate this story to all boys who have never been expelled. May all those to whom it is dedicated read it.

P. B.

CONTENTS.

—o—

CHAP.		PAGE
I. CHASSEZ-CROISEZ!		13
II. EASTCOTE,		22
III. THE FIGHT AT THE BATHING COVE,		30
IV. THE NEW BOY,		39
V. THE 'CHEQUERS,'		51
VI. GORE IN TROUBLE,		64
VII. A VISIT TO THE SPINNEY,		74
VIII. A QUARREL AND ITS CONSEQUENCES,		87
IX. A STEP TOO FAR,		98
X. HOIST WITH HIS OWN PETARD,		108
XI. THE LAST,		113

EXPELLED.

——o——

CHAPTER I.

'CHASSEZ-CROISEZ!'

IT was a hot afternoon in August. The lavatory of Eastcote School was the scene of unwonted uproar. Emerton, a tall, handsome boy, was engaged in fastening a white necktie. Goodman, close by him, was striving hard to impart to a pair of very red hands a cleanliness which, as a rule, was quite unknown to them. Tom Russell, a small, bright-looking lad, having just washed himself carefully, was endeavouring to make his shoes shine like patent leather (which they certainly were not), quite forgetting that the operation would necessitate another application of the soap and water.

At last all the rubbing was over, and the three boys commenced the important operation of brushing their hair. Goodman found that his persisted in standing up like a mop, Emerton thereupon suggesting to him that he should stand on his head in order to make it lie down. Goodman did not take Emerton's chaff in good part, for he was painfully conscious that he was about as ungainly a boy as could well be imagined. He had an unpleasant habit of continually growing out of his clothes; his collars were always a size too small, and nearly choked him, making his face redder than it was even by nature; his gloves were never fastened, and not infrequently had a big slit down the back.

'Now then,' cried Emerton, 'hurry up! We shall have to start in two minutes, and you fellows are not half ready.'

'Wait a second!' cried Goodman, trying hard to push his hand into his lavender glove, and fearing every moment to hear the ominous pop which would demonstrate that his efforts had been only too successful.

'Now then, you Tom,' called Emerton, 'go and get my hat.'

Tom obeyed. It seemed to be his function to obey, and he appeared quite resigned to it.

What was the cause of these unusual ablutions in the middle of the day? How was it that these boys, who generally at four o'clock in the afternoon were more or less muddy, should find themselves before a looking-glass, doing all they could to make themselves presentable?

This was the secret. It was the first afternoon on which Mr. Wiggins's dancing-class was to be held. Hitherto the boys had grown up ignorant of that elegant art, but Mr. Wiggins had recently determined that the village of

Eastcote should lack no longer a professor of that accomplishment which imparts ease to the movements, according to the authority of Pope. So once a week he made a descent from a neighbouring county town, and taught the youths and maidens of the village what he knew of deportment and dancing, holding a separate class for the Eastcote School. Only four of the boys were permitted to attend,—the three we have already named, and Rickards. Rickards was a day-boy, and his absence from the lavatory is therefore accounted for. He was to join the others at the small room hired by Mr. Wiggins behind the stationer's shop; his sister, Florence Rickards, who was a great friend of Cissie Russell, Tom's sister, was also to be a pupil. Tom and Cissie, however, did not go together; Cissie arrived in the charge of her mother, the wife of the headmaster of Eastcote, Dr. Russell.

Behold now the dancing-class assembled, our three friends and the two young ladies, aged respectively nine and ten. Shy enough they all looked, with the exception of Emerton. He had the airs of a small man of the world, and was accustomed to this kind of thing.

Goodman, on the other hand, felt like the proverbial bull in a china shop. He had never been to a dance in his life, and knew no more about *chassez-croisez* or the first position than he did of Sanskrit.

Tom Russell looked upon the whole affair as a big joke. He came into the room brimful of good nature and good humour, expecting to have a long half hour of fun. He did not see his sister very often, and one of the greatest treats in his life was to meet her. Next to meeting her, he liked to meet her friend Florrie, who was quite unaware of the interest he took in her.

'Good afternoon, young gentlemen,' said Mr. Wiggins, with a smile, as the boys entered. 'You see the young ladies have arrived before you.'

Tom giggled; Goodman twisted his thumbs; Emerton said, 'It is our misfortune, not our fault.' Tom looked astonished, and Goodman envious.

'Now, gentlemen,' said Mr. Wiggins, drawing himself up to his full height—five feet six—and giving a preliminary flourish on his kit, 'we will begin. In dancing, as in everything else, there must be a beginning. Please imitate my movements; stand upright, in an attitude firm, yet graceful; easy, and yet dignified.' So saying, he drew himself into what is known as the first position. Emerton, although seeming to consider it rather *infra dig.*, imitated him successfully.

Goodman tried his best to do the same, but looked about as awkward as a raw recruit when attempting the goose-step for the first time.

Tom got his wrong foot in front, looked at his sister, and began to laugh.

'Very good indeed, gentlemen,' said Mr. Wiggins encouragingly, but, at the same time, going to Goodman, he placed one arm to the right, and another to the left, giving him a slight touch under the chin to make him elevate his head.

'A little more ease,' he said to that bashful youth,— more grace. A slight smile gives an additional charm to the countenance.'

For some minutes Mr. Wiggins carefully showed the three boys how to stand. Tom, however, soon came to temporary grief. In trying to change from the first position to the second somewhat too rapidly, he came in contact with Goodman. Goodman, who had quite as much as he could do to keep himself from falling over in the constrained position he was obliged to occupy, over-toppled, and cannoned against Emerton.

'I wish to goodness you would mind what you are up to!' said that youth. 'Can't you stand on one leg for a moment? I should have thought any goose could do that.'

'You shut up!' returned Goodman, with a fierce look.

'Gentlemen, gentlemen!' remonstrated Mr. Wiggins. Goodman subsided, Emerton contenting himself with a supercilious sneer. Tom was disappointed; he had hoped that this little incident might entail a row, and Tom, like most schoolboys, was never so pleased as when a row was imminent. However, for this time, his wish was not gratified, and the lesson went slowly on.

Mr. Wiggins was patient and firm. However, after a quarter of an hour's hard work, he told them that they might rest for a minute whilst he took the young ladies in hand. Goodman and Tom were glad enough to do so, and Emerton lounged against the door in the most approved fashion, whilst Florrie and Cissie moved to the centre of the room. It was pretty evident that they had been practising alone before the boys arrived, for they knew all about the positions, and when they were uncertain of any step they did not cannon against each other like falling ninepins, as the boys had done, but moved gracefully and easily, even when incorrectly.

Tom looked on in admiration; Goodman felt more unhappy than ever, for the thought struck him that very soon he would have to dance with one of these girls, and what would happen then he shuddered to think.

B

'Now, gentlemen,' said Mr. Wiggins, 'will you join the ladies?'

They moved forward, but that was all.

'Allow me to show you how you should approach a lady in a ball-room; watch me carefully.'

The little professor then walked slowly forward, 'with a crook in his back,' as Tom whispered to Goodman. Bowing low before Cissie, he said, in a tone of honey, 'May I have the pleasure of your hand in the next quadrille, Miss Russell?'

Miss Russell did not reply; perhaps she was scarcely expected to. Mr. Wiggins suddenly straightened himself, turned to the boys, and said,—

'That is how you should do. Now, will you try, Mr. Goodman?'

Goodman felt very flattered at being addressed as 'Mr.'; he wished, however, he had not been pitched upon to make the first experiment, but there was no help for it. He pulled himself together, shuffled forward, and—then forgot what he had to say. Tom, who had been vainly trying to bottle up a laugh for the last five minutes, here exploded. Goodman turned sharply round, and made a step towards him, which had plenty of firmness in it, if lacking in grace, and was about to administer condign punishment, but Tom slipped out of his reach.

'Come, come, sir!' said Mr. Wiggins; 'please remember ladies are present.'

Goodman blushed more than ever, and turned away.

'You try, Mr. Emerton,' said Mr. Wiggins, turning to that youth.

Emerton fulfilled his duty with ease, although, as Tom

remarked with a frown, instead of addressing himself to Cissie, he spoke to Florence.

Tom then made an attempt to follow his example, and succeeded pretty well, except that at the critical moment of requesting the pleasure he burst out again into laughter.

'You mustn't,' said Cissie, with a frown.

Tom sobered as well as he could, although his face still bore more than the slight smile recommended by the professor.

'Now, gentlemen, I will instruct you how to hold a lady. Take her right hand in your left; do not press it, simply hold it. Pass your right hand gently behind her waist. No, no, Master Russell! do not grasp her as if she were a cricket-bat.'

Tom, whose laugh was very easily started, almost exploded again. Mr. Wiggins was not angry this time, because the little joke was his own. It seemed very odd to Tom to be standing there holding his sister in that fashion; it all seemed so comical. Florence too appeared rather uneasy in the hands of Emerton; she was not accustomed to have a boy's arm round her waist. However, she underwent the singular operation with considerable *sang froid*. Goodman was out of it, and was standing alone near the wall; however, he soon had a companion. The door again opened, and Rickards appeared; he had been detained by the breaking of a link of his cuff, and had been obliged to make shift with a paper-fastener instead. He entered the room with a rush, but started back surprised at the tableau presented. He had reckoned on the pleasure of dancing with Cissie, for whom he had a great, but hitherto disguised admiration; judge then of his feelings when Mr. Wiggins said,—

'We are unfortunately, gentlemen, short of ladies this afternoon. Will you, Mr. Rickards, play the part of a lady, and let Mr. Goodman be the gentleman?'

Rickards blushed; he was not yet beyond the blushing stage. Goodman felt relieved; as long as he had a boy in his grasp he was fairly at home; he seized Rickards by the hand, and put his arm well round his waist, as if he was about to begin a wrestling match. But Mr. Wiggins soon put that matter right, and then stepped back some yards in order to contemplate the scene before him. It certainly was comical enough, but he did not view it in that light.

'Yes, gentlemen, I think that will do. We are not far enough advanced to try dancing in couples this afternoon, so I think now you had better separate again.'

'Well, this is precious slow,' remarked Emerton under his breath. Tom looked up with admiration; he only wished he could look upon the whole affair in the light in which Emerton regarded it. To his youthful mind Emerton was the perfection of a swell; he did everything so easily, and as if it came by nature. Tom was painfully aware of the fact that everything he was told to do went against the grain, and it was only when he was involved in mischief that he felt at his ease.

The half-hour soon sped away. At its close Mr. Wiggins professed himself so pleased with their progress that once more he told the gentlemen to advance and claim their partners. This time Goodman was detailed to dance with Florence, much to Tom's chagrin. Emerton also had promised himself the pleasure of once more standing beside her, and was not pleased to see Goodman in his place; still less pleased was he when Goodman, by

an unfortunate accident, managed to put his far from light
foot on Florence's shoe. Florence started back with a
little cry of pain.

Emerton could not refrain from calling out,—

' You clumsy lout ! can't you see what you are doing ? '

'Don't you call me names ! ' retorted Goodman angrily;
and, dropping Florence entirely, he turned round to
Emerton. Evidently his blood was up ; throughout the
afternoon he had been painfully comparing himself with
Emerton, and becoming more angry every minute, and
now that he heard himself called a ' lout ' in the presence
of the girls, he could no longer contain himself.

' I will smash your head in if you can't keep a civil
tongue in it,' he called out in a rage.

The two girls ran to each other, expecting that something
dreadful was going to happen. No elderly lady was present, for Mrs. Russell had retired some minutes previously. However, Mr. Wiggins threw oil on the troubled
waters :—

' Come, come, gentlemen ! ' he said insinuatingly ; ' please
keep your temper. Remember, ladies are present.'

This seemed to be one of his favourite phrases. At all
events it was sufficient for this occasion, for Goodman
dropped his hand, which he had raised threateningly, and
turned sulkily away. Emerton took no notice of the out-
burst of passion, and a few minutes afterwards the boys
were dismissed, Mrs. Russell returning to take charge of
Cissie as they ran down-stairs.

CHAPTER II.

EASTCOTE.

EASTCOTE SCHOOL was presided over by Dr. Russell. It was a private school, consisting of thirty boarders and twenty-five day - boys. According to the prospectus, it was beautifully situated on the healthiest part of the sea coast.

Emerton was by common consent considered the 'cock of the school;' he was the cleverest boy in it, and first at most of the sports. He had had no rival for more than a year, but lately Goodman had shot up wonderfully from a small sturdy boy to a tall lad. He, more than any other, had suffered from Emerton's tyranny when he was small, but his opinion had of late grown stronger that the time was drawing near when he would no longer endure the airs

which Emerton gave himself. He quite believed he
could lick him now if he tried, and he wanted an occasion
for trying to present itself. The incident at the dancing-
class had given him a chance which he was not inclined
to let slip; though he said nothing as the boys walked
back to the school-house.

During tea-time he was concocting a scheme of vengeance for the insult put upon him by Emerton. He
consulted with Webb, one of his chums, a small boy, who
was one of the ringleaders in every kind of mischief.
Webb, on hearing the whole story, strongly advised him
to challenge Emerton to fight, and said that he could not
possibly pass over the insult which had been given him.

'It is not,' said the small boy, 'as if he had called you
a lout *here;* that you might have passed over; but when
other people are present no fellow can stand a thing like
that.'

Goodman had considerable respect for Webb's opinion,
for Webb was at Eastcote preparing to go to Harrow when
he was fourteen, and had a big brother there already, so
his opinion on matters of school etiquette and honour of
course carried great weight.

'I believe I could lick him,' said Goodman, bending
his arm and feeling his muscle.

'Why, of course you could!' returned Webb; 'he has
not fought any one for more than a year, and you have
had lots of fighting.'

This was quite true. Goodman was always getting
into scrapes, and was only too ready to resort to the ordeal
of battle.

Tea and prayers were over, and the evening had set in.
From seven till half-past eight was the time of prepara-

tion of lessons for the succeeding day. The boarders were
all assembled in the schoolroom at their desks, whilst at his
high desk in the corner sat one of the masters—on this
occasion, Mr. Black. Preparation-time, however, was not
very strictly observed, Mr. Black holding the view that if
a boy could prepare his lessons in an hour, he might use
the remainder of his time as he liked, as long as he did
not disturb the others. So there was a good deal of
miscellaneous reading and writing going on, many of the
boys taking advantage of the master's leniency to neglect
their lessons almost entirely, if they had anything else
they wanted to do. Of course they suffered for this on
the succeeding day, but that was their own look-out.

On this particular evening, Goodman failed to attend to
his work at all. He and Webb employed themselves in
the composition of an elaborate challenge to Emerton.
The first draft was not satisfactory, and was torn up,
but the second one seemed to meet the case. It ran as ·
follows :—

'I will fight you any time this week, down at the
village. You called me a clumsy lout. I will show you
that French polish is not going to have its own way in
everything.'

The meaning was clear enough, although the expression
of it was certainly a little mixed. The paper was neatly
folded, and addressed to

'C. EMERTON, ESQUIRE,'

for in a formal challenge like this it was felt that no point
of etiquette must be neglected. The next point was to
get the challenge delivered. Webb flatly refused to have
any hand in that; so Goodman handed it to Tom, who
was sitting next to him.

It was Tom's unhappy fate to be always chosen for unpleasant duties of this kind. He was the son of the headmaster, and, as such, was popularly supposed to be able to run any risks without danger. Unfortunately for Tom this was quite a mistake, for Dr. Russell, when he placed his son in his own school, resolved that he should be treated exactly the same as any other boy; in fact, in the fear of being thought to act partially towards his son, he was more than usually harsh to him. The consequence was, that between his schoolfellows and his father Tom had rather a bad time of it. However, on the present occasion he did not make any objection to carrying the precious missive. In the first place, he guessed what it was, and looked forward with pleasurable anticipation to the coming row between the two big boys. Besides, he well knew that, had he refused to carry it, Goodman would inevitably have licked him on the first opportunity; so, under the pretext of wanting to ask Mr. Black a question, he went up to his desk, and, as he returned, slipped the challenge on Emerton's desk in front of him, and then resumed his place, watching carefully the effect of his action.

Emerton took up the note, read it, drew a piece of paper out of his case, scribbled a couple of words upon it, and flipped it carelessly across the room. It fell near Webb, who picked it up and handed it to Goodman; it simply contained the words, 'All right.' Mr. Black, however, had witnessed the action, and had noticed also what Tom had done.

'Bring me that paper, Emerton,' he said. Emerton looked up and saw the master's eye fixed on him. There was no help for it. He took the challenge up to Mr.

Black, who read it, crumpled it up, and threw it in the fireplace. He did not say anything then, but Goodman's feelings were far from comfortable.

Preparation was over at last.

'Goodman, stay behind!' cried Mr. Black. Goodman obeyed, retaining his seat, while the others poured out of the room on their way to their bedrooms.

'Did you write that note?' asked Mr. Black.

'Yes, sir,' said Goodman.

'What does this mean?' inquired the master.

Goodman made no reply.

'Write me out one hundred lines,' said Mr. Black. 'Now you can go to bed. I shall have my eye on you during the next few days.'

Goodman slunk off, feeling, if possible, still more incensed against Emerton, who, as he not unnaturally thought, had purposely left the note lying on his desk.

'Look here, you young beggar!' said Emerton to Tom as they reached the dormitory; 'I will teach you to bring cheeky notes to me.'

He caught him by the arm and boxed his ears, Tom making futile efforts to escape.

'It wasn't my fault,' pleaded Tom; 'he would have licked me if I had not brought it.'

'And I have licked you now that you have brought it,' responded Emerton complacently, letting him go with a final kick. Nevertheless Tom bore it with equanimity, for he knew now that the fight must come off sooner or later, and he was almost the only boy in possession of the important news, a fact which raised his estimation of himself considerably.

Before five minutes had passed, pretty nearly all the

boys were aware of the challenge, and various opinions were expressed as to the result of the coming combat. Most of the boys were by no means sorry that Goodman had at last plucked up courage to oppose Emerton, for many of them had suffered from his tyranny in times past.

'He's a good deal too cheeky,' was a small boy's remark; 'he's always punching a fellow's head for nothing. I hope Goodman will lick him.'

Webb, it was noticed, did not take any part in the discussion; the fact was, that he was a very cautious lad, and wished to see the result of the fight before throwing in his lot with either of the two sections.

Tom really did not care which won, for he was more or less bullied by both. Perhaps he hated Emerton the most, for he envied as well as disliked him. He did his lessons without an effort; he was at the head of the school, and he would win the single scholarship of which Eastcote boasted. He did not crib, because there was no need; he had no rival worth thinking of. Rickards was the only one who could run him at all close, and he was a day-boy, and, as such, ineligible for this particular prize. Goodman, although as big, was far down in the school; another reason why he hated Emerton. Tom was generally at the bottom of his class; he had so many punishments that he generally had to employ his preparation time in doing them, a course of conduct which entailed a further series of punishments the next day.

It had soon become known amongst the day-boys that Goodman had been guilty of the tremendous effrontery of challenging Emerton. Their only fear was, that the encounter might take place without their knowledge.

They knew well enough that it must be held in the village, out of the school precincts, for there was no corner of the playground sufficiently far removed from the house for it to take place there in safety; but they were afraid the secret of the meeting might be kept, and that they would not see any of the fun.

By the school rules, the boys were allowed twice a week to have an hour and a half free in the village, to do just

as they liked, permission being first obtained. Of course it was during this much-valued holiday that all the fights took place. However, this outing was dependent on good conduct. No boy might go into the village unless he had finished up all his punishments; this put off all chance of a fight for at least a week, for Goodman had several punishments on hand, in addition to the one he had received for sending the challenge.

'What an awful nuisance it is!' said Webb. 'As likely as not they will make it up before the week is out.'

'That will never do,' replied Mason. 'We must help Goodman. Black won't care who does the lines, as long as they are done. I'll do fifty, if you will.'

Webb agreed, for he was very anxious that the fight should take place. Goodman for once found his friends only too ready to do him a service, and, although he knew that they did it for selfish reasons, he was not at all sorry to get his punishments done by proxy.

At the close of morning school he walked up to Emerton and said,—

'Will to-morrow afternoon do for you?'

'Any time you like,' replied Emerton; 'it will be equally agreeable to me.'

'I hope you may find it so,' retorted Goodman.

'You may be quite certain I shall,' returned he; 'it is always good fun to me to lick impertinent cads.'

Goodman looked for a moment as if he were about to anticipate the next day's encounter; but he restrained himself and said, 'I will smash you to a jelly for that.'

'All right!' said Emerton; 'you can try to-morrow.'

CHAPTER III

THE FIGHT AT THE BATHING COVE.

'THERE, Goodie!' exclaimed Tom; 'there's fifty lines for you, and if you win you will have to pay them back to me next time I get into a row.' Goodman did not reply, although he accepted the gift.

He made an awful hash of his lessons that morning, for the important event was to come off in the afternoon.

The boys found their way down to the well-known spot —the bathing cove—in small bodies of three or four, so as not to create suspicion.

Rarely in the history of the school had punishments been wiped off with such rapidity; every boy was anxious to be on the scene of action. Day-boys turned out in considerable force, forgetting everything else in the all-absorbing theme of the great conflict at hand. The spot selected was certainly retired enough; it was cut off from the bathing cove by a line of rocks; the sand was hard and firm at low water.

In a few minutes an impromptu ring was formed, and round this gathered the interested spectators. It was discovered that by some oversight neither of the principals had a second.

'Here, you Webb!' said Emerton; 'you be my second.'

'Very well, Emerton,' responded Webb, although he would very gladly have been excused.

Goodman looked round to see whom he should ask, for no one volunteered; there was not a boy who was not afraid to do so for fear of the subsequent vengeance of Emerton, should he win.

'Now, young Tom,' said Goodman, 'you come and be my second, or else I'll '— He left the threat unfinished, and Tom, to his great disgust, had to come forward.

The two big boys took off their coats, waistcoats, and collars, and faced each other in the diminutive ring. Time-keepers were not appointed. The fact was, that a regular fight was of such rare occurrence at Eastcote that formalities of this description were generally omitted.

Rickards gave the word, and the combatants doubled their fists and advanced slowly towards each other.

Fighting is not a pleasant thing. It is often said that it is best for boys who have a quarrel to fight—that it lets off bad blood—that they can shake hands after it and be better friends than ever. That may be the case some-times, but for once that it may let off a little bad blood, it engenders more a dozen times. As long as boys are boys, fighting will probably be more or less frequent amongst them, but the rarer it is the better.

It is one's lower nature that comes to the top on

such occasions — one's better feelings for the time are entirely crushed. A fight in a good cause is truly noble, but in a bad cause it is about the worst thing one can undertake.

Unfortunately, on the present occasion, the cause was undoubtedly bad, and no one but an unthinking lad could have looked with any pleasure on the struggle that now took place.

In ten minutes it was evident that Goodman's strength would not be of much avail against Emerton's superior skill. At the first, the big boy had the advantage, but very soon Tom found that his man was getting more and more unwilling to come to the scratch, whilst Emerton seemed almost as fresh as ever. When a man loses heart he loses half his strength, and Goodman soon seemed to feel that his chance of success was but small; he fought aimlessly and wildly, and floundered about on the deeply trampled sand, several times measuring his length on it. In less than a quarter of an hour it was all over, and Tom had the unpleasant duty of doing what he could to aid the vanquished.

Emerton apparently had sustained little damage—his nose was bleeding, but that was soon stopped. Goodman, although showing but few signs of injury, was badly hurt about the body; he was panting, both with rage and from want of breath, and in reply to Tom's query as to how he felt, he merely vouchsafed a surly 'Never you mind.'

'There, that will do,' said Emerton to Webb, who was wiping the blood from his face with a wet handkerchief; 'I am all right now. The sooner some of you fellows get back home the better.'

' I am jolly glad you've won ! ' said Webb ; ' I thought you would.'

' Yes ; I guess I have done for that lout now,' replied he, putting his coat on and commencing to walk towards the school.

As he passed Goodman, he stopped for a moment.

' I hope you are satisfied,' he said.

Goodman gave a surly growl in reply.

' Perhaps this will be a lesson to you how to behave to your betters,' continued Emerton, and then walked on, with a small crowd of admirers at his heels.

Goodman soon followed him, taking Tom's arm unwillingly.

' It's all your fault, you young beggar,' he said ; ' if you'd backed me up a little better, I believe I should have licked him.'

' Oh no, you wouldn't,' said Tom cheerily ; ' he'd the best of it all along, I could see.'

' No, he hadn't,' returned Goodman. ' I'll punch your head if you can't keep a civil tongue in your mouth.'

Tom thought this rather hard, considering he had been his second against his will.

Just then Mason came up.

' Hallo, Goodie ! ' he remarked ; ' you won't look so handsome as usual next time you go to the dancing-class.'

Goodman made a savage hit at him, but missed. Tom burst out laughing, and in a moment received a tremendous blow from the vanquished would-be champion which laid him flat on the sand. Directly he rose he ran off as hard as he could, leaving Goodman to find his way home alone.

'I say, Tom,' remarked Mason, a few days later, as they were both wandering about the playground, 'my cousin's coming here next week.'

'Who is he?' inquired Tom.

'He's called Gore,' was the reply.   'I haven't seen him for a long time, but he used to be a jolly fellow.'

'Will he be in the eleven?' asked Tom, who had hopes of being soon elected into the team.

'I should think so,' replied the other; 'why, he is more than sixteen.'

Poor Tom's countenance fell, for he saw that his chance of promotion was indefinitely postponed.

'Never mind,' said Mason; 'some fellows are sure to go at the end of the term, and you are safe to be in the eleven next season.'

A sudden thought struck Tom.

'Is he as big as Emerton?' he asked.

'I don't know, I'm sure; I haven't seen him for such an awful time; but I hope he is.'

Tom acquiesced in this hope, for, although less than a week had elapsed since the big fight, most of the boys had had cause to regret that Emerton had been victorious. His behaviour had become simply unbearable; none of the masters had such authority as he had, at least out of the school.   He carried his tyranny to an extreme point, bullying nearly every one without distinction, till some of the smaller boys had almost determined to form a society for his suppression; but there was a difficulty in managing it, for Emerton was skilful enough to carry on his tyranny when but few were present.

As the two small boys were talking of him, he came up.

'Here, you Tom!' he said sharply; 'I want you to go

down to the village and fetch my big knife; it's being ground at Smith's, you know, the ironmonger's.'

'Don't you wish you may get it!' said Tom. 'I got into an awful row last week for breaking bounds, and I'm not going to chance it again.'

'Breaking bounds' was a great offence at Eastcote. Dr. Russell considered that he gave the boys quite as much liberty as was good for them, and any one who was rash enough to visit the village at forbidden hours was considered to have committed one of the gravest offences against school discipline. Notwithstanding the fear of subsequent severe punishment, breaking bounds was a transgression which frequently was committed, and Tom had on many occasions been obliged to make a furtive excursion at prohibited times. However, he had now determined that he would not run the risk any more, at all events for the present.

'What do you mean, you young beggar?' exclaimed Emerton, in reply to Tom's speech.

'If you want to go, go yourself,' replied Tom pluckily, at the same time keeping well out of Emerton's reach.

'That's right, Tom!' chimed in Mason, backing him up manfully.

At this juncture Webb appeared on the scene. Since the fight he had attached himself to Emerton, and the two were rarely apart; he performed the function of a parasite to a patron.

'Here, Webb!' called out Emerton; 'just catch that Tom for me, and kick him.'

Webb hastened to obey, for he was bigger than Tom, and knew from long experience that he would have no difficulty in this case. Emerton seized Mason, and held him back, in order that he might not interpose; but Tom's blood was up, and he refused to be licked. Breaking from Webb's grasp, after giving him one blow, he ran as hard as he could towards the middle of the playground, where stood the giant's stride. Seizing a rope in his hands and the pole with his legs, he rapidly swarmed up to the top. Webb did his best to pull the rope from under him; but Tom's grasp was too sure, and he was soon completely out of reach.

'Hallo!' sang out Ellis, who was near. 'Go it, Tom!'

Other boys quickly gathered round, and incited Webb to follow Tom up the pole. This was not quite what Webb wanted to do, but he could not show the white feather in the presence of so many, so he commenced to swarm upwards. However, Tom had decidedly the advantage, and, seizing the rope by which Webb was climbing, he shook it so fiercely that Webb could make no headway at all, and soon dropped to the ground again.

'All right!' he shouted. 'I'll soon fetch you out of that. Here you are, everybody! take cock-shots at him.'

This proposal was received with acclamation, and Tom soon had cause to regret that he had climbed into such deceptive safety. Balls and pebbles flew around him; he couldn't retaliate, and had to dodge the missiles as best he might. Emerton and Goodman, who had now joined the throng, laughing loudly, urged the youngsters to continue the fun. Tom saw that his position was becoming untenable. He seized a loose rope, and, swinging it round, soon cleared a vacant circle of several feet. But this did not avail him much; and before long Webb had seized the rope which he was swinging, and held on to it; other boys seized the remaining ropes, and Tom had now no means of defence. However, he managed to jerk one rope from the hands of a small boy, and, swinging this viciously round, he hit Webb on the head with the wooden handle attached to it. Webb dropped to the ground as if he had been shot. In another moment Tom was on the ground beside him, fearing that he had killed him.

'Get some water!' he shouted excitedly, as he knelt beside the prostrate boy.

'Oh, bosh!' said Mason. 'He isn't hurt; he's only shamming.'

To Tom's immense relief Webb opened his eyes and got up.

All the boys were so intent on the occurrence that no one noticed that Dr. Russell was crossing the playground to see what was causing all this commotion, and before any one knew of his approach he was in the centre of the group.

'What's this?' he asked severely; 'has any one fallen from the giant's stride?'

'No, sir,' replied Emerton; 'but Webb has been hurt by one of the ropes hitting him.'

'Who did it?' further inquired the Doctor. Tom was obliged to reply.

'Please, sir, I did.'

'By accident, I presume?'

'Partly, sir,' said Tom.

'What do you mean?' was the natural inquiry.

'I was swinging it round, sir, and it hit him on the head.'

The defence was a very weak one, and Tom felt it to be so. He further *knew* it was the moment after, when the Doctor stalked away, leaving Tom with enough work on his hands to last for a couple of days. He slowly followed his father towards the schoolroom, Mason accompanying him, leaving Webb rubbing a bump on his head the size of a pigeon's egg.

'I say, Tom, that's precious hard lines,' said Mason. ' If I'd been you, I'd have told him how it was.'

'Oh, never mind,' rejoined Tom. ' I don't care much, now that I've given that fellow something to remember.'

'I almost thought you'd done for him, though,' said Mason.

'So did I,' returned Tom, with a shudder, as he remembered his sensations when he saw Webb fall ; 'I'm jolly glad I didn't. But if that Emerton thinks I'm going to go down to the village just when he chooses, he is very much mistaken. I shan't.'

'No more will I,' said Mason. 'I hope to goodness, when my cousin comes, that he will be able to back me up and beat that fellow. Emerton seems as if he never could have enough of kicking me. One of these days I mean to see if his shins are made of cast-iron.'

CHAPTER IV.

THE NEW BOY.

DR. RUSSELL was an old Cambridge man, and in his time had been second wrangler. One of his old college chums was Mr. Gore, who was now a lawyer in large practice. He intended to send his son to Cambridge, but, finding that at the school at which he had been placed mathematics was not made a prominent feature of instruction, he had determined that he would place him under his old friend for a year or so previous to sending him to college.

39

It thus came to pass that Charlie Gore, at the age of sixteen, was placed at a fresh school. He scarcely liked this himself, but his father seemed to imagine that Dr. Russell's tutorship would be of such advantage to him that he willingly acquiesced in the arrangement.

To the surprise of the school, on Monday morning they found that there was an addition to their number. Just as school opened, Dr. Russell walked into the room, followed by a fine young fellow, of upright and manly bearing. The Doctor took the unusual course of introducing the new-comer to the class under his care.

'Boys, I have brought you a new companion. I am sure you will find him a valuable addition to your number, both in school and out of it.'

The boys grinned rather helplessly—they did not quite know what to say. Emerton, who usually took the lead on such occasions, was silent likewise, but from the frown which gathered over his face it was easy to observe that the new-comer was far from being welcome as regarded himself.

'There he is,' whispered Mason to Tom. 'Isn't he a jolly-looking fellow?'

'First-rate,' said Tom. 'I should think he could knock Emerton into a cocked hat.'

'I only hope he will,' returned Mason. 'Look here! let's have a lark. I'm going to write a note to Emerton, and you do so too; we will write alternate words, so that he won't be able to tell who they come from.'

This idea commended itself to Tom's mind. Phillips was taken into the secret, with several others. A number of little cocked-hat notes were dropped before Emerton's desk at various times during the morning, or slipped slyly into his books. As he opened them he seemed to grow more and more angry. The first one ran thus:—

'This will put your nose out of joint, won't it?'

Needless to say the note was anonymous.

'Don't show the white feather,' ran another; and a third bolder still,—

'Shall I be your second down at the bathing cove?'

And so on.

Before school was over, however, Emerton had quite recovered himself, and as the bell rang for breaking up he walked over to Gore, and, taking his arm, led him for a stroll round the playground.

'I hope you'll find it all right here,' he said, in a friendly tone. 'It's rather a hole, but we don't have bad times sometimes. There's some very decent bathing, and our eleven this half is a very tolerable one. You play cricket of course?'

'A little,' replied Gore; 'but I've been going in for exams. so much lately that I am fearfully out of practice. However, I mean to play as much as I can for the next few months.'

'Do you swim?' asked Emerton.

'Oh yes; I can swim fairly well,' was the reply.

'It must be rather a bore for you to come here. I should have thought you would have been leaving school about now. How old are you?' inquired Emerton.

'I'm sixteen and a bit,' Gore answered. 'I've only come here for mathematics, I believe.'

'Well, you'll find the old boy tremendous on that; if he had his way he'd try to make senior wranglers of us all, but I don't think he will succeed very soon. Come and let's have an hour's practice before dinner.'

'All right,' said Gore; 'but I want to see one of the fellows here first, as I know something of him. Oh, there he is!'

Emerton watched him with some curiosity as he ran across the playground towards little Mason, who was quite proud to be seen shaking hands with the new fellow.

'How are you, young un?' said Gore. 'I haven't seen you for an awful time. I believe you were in knickerbockers when you last came down to my place.'

'Yes,' said Mason; 'but please don't let the other fellows here know that I am your cousin.'

'Why not?' asked Gore, with a laugh. 'Are you ashamed of me?'

'No, but they'll think I shall sneak to you about everything if they know, so I don't want you to be too kind to me,—at least, not when other fellows are looking.'

'Oh, you don't?' said Gore, with a smile. 'All right then, look out!' and, before Mason knew what he was about, Gore had tossed him over his shoulder, and was running with him towards the wickets.

'Oh, please, Gore, let me down! My head's coming off!' yelled the youngster.

'Now then, you go and back stop,' said Gore; 'and if you let a ball pass, see if I don't take it out of you.'

Mason ran away to his place, feeling happier than he had done for a long time, for he saw that his cousin was the same as he had known him years before—a jolly sort of fellow, always ready to do a good turn to another, even although that other was a diminutive and not particularly respectable little chap.

Emerton's spirits revived during the next half-hour; he found that Gore had spoken the strict truth when he said that he did not play cricket much; he clean bowled him three times, whilst Gore could make no impression on his wicket. Several of the boys gathered round to watch, for they felt considerable curiosity in reference to the prowess of the new-comer. Goodman was looking on with savage satisfaction, comparing carefully the apparent strength of his enemy and the new-comer.

'I say, Goodie,' whispered Tom, as he stood beside him, 'I think the new fellow will have the best of it; don't you?'

'I hope so,' returned Goodman. 'It will serve that fellow precious right if Gore knocks him out of time!'

Poor Goodman for the last ten days had felt fearfully out of it; no boy paid him the slightest respect, and if he tried to bully a youngster he would immediately retort by threatening to tell Emerton. Moreover, Emerton lost no opportunity of showing how he despised him. However, his defeat had been too severe for him to be able to contemplate a renewal of the struggle, and in consequence he had been spending a miserable time, brooding over his lost opportunity, and wishing that he had postponed for another year his endeavour to become cock of the school.

'There goes the bell,' said Emerton at last; 'I'll give you one ball more.'

'Fire away!' replied Gore, who was at the wicket; 'let's have one more chance of a slog!'

Emerton bowled a swift, long pitch; it went to leg; Gore swiped round and caught it just as it rose. It was a tremendous hit, and the ball flew clean out of the ground, over the hedge and into the little stream which ran at the back of the ground.

'Hallo! that's gone,' said Mason. 'I can't field that, anyhow.'

'In you go!' cried Tom; 'you'll be late if you don't.'

He set the example by running as hard as he could towards the house, followed by the others more slowly.

'That's a nuisance,' said Gore. 'I suppose that's gone for ever.'

'I'm afraid so,' replied Emerton; 'but it doesn't make much difference; we can get a new one down in the village.'

'That's all right,' said Gore. 'I'll go down and get one some time this afternoon.'

'Thanks,' said Emerton. 'We make it a rule here that whoever loses a ball gets a new one; I thought I might as well tell you.'

'Oh, of course!' said Gore. 'I'll go down after afternoon school.'

Gore was ignorant of the fact that to visit the village without special permission was a heinous offence.

'I think I've got him,' said Emerton to himself. 'It won't be a good beginning for him to be caught breaking bounds.'

Afternoon school was nearly over; the boys were getting more and more tired; the hum of voices became weaker and weaker, and anxious looks towards the clock more frequent.

'I say, Tom,' whispered Mason, 'can you see the clock? I can't from here.'

'Yes,' replied Tom; 'it's five minutes to four.'

'It ought to be ashamed of itself,' said Mason, 'going so slowly. I believe the old thing is stopped.'

'Yes, it is ashamed of itself,' said Tom, giggling to himself as he remembered an old riddle. 'It's got its hands before its face.'

Mason, to whom the joke was new, almost burst out laughing, but restrained himself as he saw Mr. Black's eye on him.

'Are you going down to the village after school?' he asked.

'No,' said Tom, turning at once from joyousness to sorrow. 'I've got no end of work to do; I shall have to stick indoors for the next couple of days.'

'Well, I'm off,' said Mason. 'Directly the clock strikes I shall strike too.'

Though this was carried on in whispers, Mr. Black was not unconscious of forbidden conversation, and Mason came very near receiving a punishment which would have put a stop to his projected expedition. However, the master was merciful for once, and a frown sufficed to bring the youngster into order. When the clock did strike he did not hesitate to take advantage of his liberty, and he was by far the first to be outside the gates and in the free air beyond.

Gore, after loitering about a few minutes, strolled complacently through the great gates, and began his first walk towards the village of Eastcote. He had seen Mason shoot out shortly before, and thought it was 'rather rum' that he had not waited for him. He made his way toward the village, intending to get the ball which he owed Emerton; he had inquired where it could be got and the price of it, and found that 2s. 8d. was the sum usually given for practice balls. They were to be obtained, as were most other articles which boys needed, at the ironmonger's. But before he sought the shop he took a short stroll along the cliff, enjoying immensely the, to him, novel sight of the sea; he watched the vessels as they sailed by, listened to the scream of the gulls as they flew overhead, and congratulated himself that he had been sent to a school at the seaside. His reverie, however, was suddenly interrupted by seeing Mason coming towards him full pelt; on reaching him he was so out of breath that he could only whisper,—

'Cave! Black's coming,' and then drop to the ground exhausted.

'What on earth's the row?' asked Gore. 'You seem to be doing a race against time, little un, and time's had the best of it.'

'Run!' said Mason, who had now partly recovered breath. 'You will be nabbed as sure as eggs.'

Gore looked up, and saw not twenty yards off the figure of Mr. Black, who was taking an afternoon stroll along the cliffs. The sight did not at all frighten him, but for some reason not apparent Mason seemed to imagine that the advent of a master would be sufficient to make him vanish as rapidly as possible.

'It's too late now,' said Mason; 'he has seen you. I wouldn't be in your shoes for a good deal.'

'I daresay not; you'd find them rather uncomfortable,' replied Gore, still further mystified. His perplexity was soon cleared up.

'How is this, Gore?' asked Mr. Black as he came up. 'Have you had permission to be out this afternoon?'

'No, sir,' he replied. 'I didn't know it was necessary to obtain any.'

'Are you then under the impression that you can

come out for a walk whenever you like ?' inquired Mr. Black.

'I'm afraid I didn't think much about it, sir; I saw some of the other boys going out into the village after school, and so I thought that I might go too.'

Mr. Black looked at him rather severely for a moment, as if doubtful whether to take his expression of ignorance as indicating the complete truth, but apparently he was satisfied with his scrutiny.

'Some one ought to have told you,' he said, in a kinder tone. 'Of course you cannot be expected to know all the rules the first day of your arrival, but ignorance is always considered a very bad defence. No one is allowed to come out into the village alone without first obtaining leave, and that is never given unless his conduct during the previous week has been in all respects satisfactory. So you see that for a week at least you must confine yourself to the precincts of the school, unless you choose to ask special permission from the Doctor himself.'

'I'm very sorry, sir,' said Gore; 'but I can assure you that it was quite a mistake on my part.'

'I am quite ready to believe you,' said Mr. Black. 'I am going back to the school now; you had better return with me.'

'Very well, sir,' said Gore.

'You have leave, of course, Mason,' said the master, turning to the smaller boy.

'Oh yes, sir,' he replied, grinning rather voluminously.

'All right; don't get into mischief now,' said Mr. Black, as he and Gore turned towards the schoolhouse.

Gore was, however, very annoyed that Emerton had not warned him that he would be transgressing the rules in going out without leave, and he determined that when he got back he would speak to him about it. On the other hand he appreciated, too, little Mason's kindness in having done what he could to save him from a row. As they passed through the gates he saw the Doctor at a front window, but the latter, seeing him accompanied by a master, of course took no notice of his return.

One of the first boys he met on reaching the playground was Emerton.

'Have you been down in the village?' he inquired.

'Yes,' replied Gore.

'Did you manage to find the shop?'

'I've not been as far as that.'

'Oh, how was that?'

'I met Mr. Black.'

'You don't say so!' exclaimed Emerton. 'What did he say?'

Gore repeated briefly what Mr. Black had told him, and left Emerton to explain.

'I'm awfully sorry!' he began; 'but I'd no idea that you didn't know the rules about going out. I thought when you said you would go down to the village after school, that of course you had asked leave or were going to do so.'

'I didn't know anything about it,' returned Gore. 'How could I?'

'Perhaps it was rather stupid of me,' assented Emerton. 'I'm awfully sorry! Don't bother any more about it; some other fellow will be sure to be going down, and if you will hand me over the cash I'll get some one to bring it up for you.'

'That'll be the best way, I think,' said Gore. 'Let me see; 2s. 8d., isn't it?'

'Yes, we make shift with those for practice.'

Gore handed over the money, leaving Emerton to arrange for its expenditure. This he soon managed. Spying Tom in a distant corner of the playground, he went towards him, calling to Webb on his way; Tom saw them coming, but was too late to escape.

'Well, what do you want now?' queried that young hero.

'I'll tell you,' said Emerton; 'you told me you were going down to the village this afternoon.'

'Yes, I know I did; but I didn't know then that I should get two hundred lines to-day, and have to stay in and write them before I can go out.'

'Why aren't you writing them now?' asked Emerton, with the tone and authority of a master.

'Because I haven't got to give them in till to-morrow afternoon,' replied Tom. 'Besides, it's no business of yours.'

'Come now, none of your cheek,' said Emerton. 'You told me you were going down, and if you choose to go and get a punishment in the meantime that's no fault of mine. You've got to go down to the village this afternoon whether you like it or no; you mustn't go and tell me lies in that way.'

'It wasn't a lie!' retorted Tom angrily. 'I wanted to go down badly enough.'

'Well, you know how to do it anyhow,' returned Emerton; 'you've had plenty of practice—you've been down for me seven or eight times this term.'

'Yes,' said Tom ruefully, 'and I've been caught twice, and if I get caught again I shall get caned as sure as life.'

D

'Well, that won't hurt me,' said Emerton, in a careless tone. ' If you've only been caught twice out of seven, the chances are two to seven that you won't be caught this time. Look here—here's 2s. 8d. ; you must go down to Smith's and get me the ball. Catch hold.'

Tom did not hold out his hand, so Emerton seized it . and forced open his closed fist, pushing the money into it; he then turned away, leaving Tom to do what he pleased. Poor fellow ! he was in a hole ; he knew well enough that if he refused to accept the commission a more than usually severe licking was in store for him, but he had manfully determined that he would not again risk breaking bounds. In a puzzled state of mind he walked across the playground, thinking that he would go indoors and get on with his punishment as fast as possible so as to be free to go down to town the next day, hoping that Emerton would accept this compromise.

CHAPTER V.

THE 'CHEQUERS.'

GORE'S unexpected appearance on the scene had made Emerton somewhat afraid that he would not 'pull off' the scholarship with the ease he had anticipated. He therefore took measures to ensure his success.

During the previous week he had persuaded Webb, with whom he had struck up a very warm friendship, to do him a great service. As has been before mentioned,

Webb had a brother at Harrow, and Emerton concluded that at Harrow, as at most large schools, 'cribs' were far from being unknown. Judging that Webb's brother would be very much of the same stamp as Webb himself, he concluded that if any 'cribs' were in use he would be sure to possess one. He had accordingly persuaded his protégé to write to his brother to lend him for a few weeks a 'crib' of Horace, the third book of which was one of the subjects of the coming exam.

'I scarcely like to ask him,' said Webb. 'I don't know if he has ever done Horace, for one thing; he was in Cicero last half.'

'Well, if he hasn't one himself he can easily borrow one if he likes, I suppose?' returned Emerton. 'Anyhow you must try; I've done you some uncommonly good turns, you know.'

'Yes, you have,' assented Webb. 'But if this business is found out I shall get into a jolly row; in fact, I expect the Doctor would expel me.'

'What if he does?' replied Emerton; 'you would only be sent to Harrow a few months earlier.'

'Yes; that's all very well for you, but I don't want to risk it.'

'But you won't risk anything,' said Emerton persuasively. 'We won't have the book sent to the school, but to some one down in the village, and then we can fetch it, and no one will know anything about it.'

After a little more persuasion Webb consented, and he wrote to his brother accordingly. He had asked him, in accordance with Emerton's advice, to send the book to the 'Chequers Inn,' addressed to him c/o William Stokes. William Stokes, more commonly known as Billy, had been till recently in the employ of Dr. Russell. He was the lad who cleaned the boots and knives, and did odd jobs about the school, but in consequence of misconduct had been summarily dismissed.

Emerton, however, was too careful to fetch the book himself, and Webb refused to do so in spite of all persuasions. So another messenger had to be found. Emerton recollected that Tom had not yet fetched the ball for which he had given him the money. He shouted to him to approach.

'When are you going to fetch that ball for me?' he asked.

'I can go to-day,' said Tom. 'I've got leave.'

'Do you mind getting a book for me as well?' asked Emerton.

'All right,' replied Tom, thankful that Emerton did not 'lick' him for postponing his visit to the ironmonger's so long.

'I'll tell you what I want you to do; I can't go and do it myself, as I've promised to go in quite another direction. You know the "Chequers"?'

'You don't want me to go there?' asked Tom anxiously.

'What are you flaring up about now? I don't want you to go in there and get anything to drink.'

'Well, but you know we aren't allowed to go into public-houses at all,' said Tom.

'Oh, nonsense! Of course I know the rule, but that means we must not go in there and get beer or anything of that sort. All I want you to do is to go in and ask for a book which belongs to Webb. You know Billy well enough?'

'Yes, I know him,' said Tom ruefully, seeing that he

was in a hole ; 'but when I promised to fetch you a book,
I never thought you meant to get it from there.'

'I can't help what you thought ; you've promised, and
you'll have to keep to it now.　You show this slip of
paper to Billy, and he will give you the book ; bring it up
to me, but don't let any fellow see you do it.　You won't
get caught ; don't be afraid ; nobody is ever near that part
of the village.　Besides, you can see them coming all
down the High Street if there's any one about.'

Tom took the slip of paper, but didn't promise to carry
out Emerton's wishes.　However, on thinking it over,
he decided that he must run the risk.　He had given his
promise, and Tom never liked breaking his word.

Emerton and Webb had arranged some time previously
to make an excursion together that same afternoon to
Hartwell Spinney.　This was a good way off ; they would
only just have time to get there and come back within
the allotted hour and a half.　When afternoon came,
Tom, much against his will, set out for the village.　The
few boys who were free that afternoon all went along the
cliffs, with the exception of Emerton and Webb, who
struck off inland ; Gore did not seem inclined to take
advantage of his liberty ; so Tom thought that not only
would no master see him, but there was no risk of even
any of his companions coming across his path.

He entered the 'Chequers' door, after giving a careful
look round, and five minutes afterwards he emerged
therefrom with the book under his arm, looking very
crestfallen.　He hadn't gone many yards before a hand
fell on his shoulder.

He started round in a fright, and almost dropped the
book.

'Oh, Gore, is it you? I'm so glad! I thought it was Mr. Black.'

'Why should you think it was Mr. Black?' asked Gore cheerily.

'I don't know,' said Tom.

'Well, I do,' remarked Gore. 'I know where you've been.'

'Oh, do you?' said Tom rather piteously. 'Don't tell.'

'Tell!' exclaimed Gore; 'what on earth should I tell for? You don't think I'm a sneak, do you?'

'Oh no! I'm sure you aren't,' said Tom effusively.

'Well, look here,' said Gore, putting his arm in the youngster's. 'All the same, I should like to know why you went in there.'

'I didn't want to go there at all.'

'Then why on earth did you?' asked Gore. 'When it comes to going into public-houses, it looks very bad, especially for such a youngster as you are. Now, what's it all about? Tell me.'

'I went in to get a book,' he replied.

'A book!' exclaimed Gore; 'that's a rum sort of place to go to in search of literature, certainly.'

'It wasn't a book for me,' exclaimed Tom; 'it was for Webb; it was a book he had had sent him.'

'I see. So Webb made you go in there? Why didn't you tell him to go himself?'

'But it wasn't Webb made me go,' said Tom, wondering how he could keep Emerton's name out of the transaction.

'Well, never mind,' said Gore kindly. 'You've done a very stupid thing, and you'd better make your mind up never to do it again.' But Tom continued his confession, and the worst part of his tale soon came out.

'They made me pay 1s. 6d. for carriage,' he said. 'Do you think that was fair?'

'One and sixpence,' exclaimed Gore, 'for a little book like that! Why, of course, it was not! Who's cheated you like that?'

'Billy,' was the reply.

'And who's Billy?'

Tom explained the antecedents of Mr. William Stokes. 'He told me the carriage was 1s. 6d.,' said Tom, 'and when I told him that I was sure it wasn't, he said, very well, I needn't take it, and that he'd let my father know

I'd been into the "Chequers" talking to him; so he made me give him 1s. 6d. so that he might not sneak about me.'

'What a young rascal it is!' exclaimed Gore angrily.

'What can I do?' asked Tom.

'You can't do much,' was Gore's reply, 'but perhaps I can work the oracle for you.'

He was thoroughly angry at the trick played on his young companion. He walked back to the 'Chequers,' entered the door, and found a lad whom he at once recognised, from the description given, as Billy, standing alone behind the bar.

'Are you Billy?' he inquired.

'Yes, I am,' was the surly reply.

'Then I want that money that Tom Russell gave you just now.'

'Oh! anything else?' replied Billy, with a wink that was meant to be confidential.

'Yes, there is something else,' said Gore. 'If you don't let me have it, I shall go straight to your master and see what he says about it.'

This threat seemed rather to frighten Billy, and he muttered something about its being a present from Master Tom, and he didn't mean any harm by taking it.

'That's enough,' said Gore shortly. 'Hand over a shilling, you can keep the sixpence for the carriage, although I believe it was carriage paid.'

It was, but Gore hadn't noticed it, and Billy didn't choose to enlighten him on this point. He handed over the shilling, and Gore speedily left the neighbourhood of the 'Chequers.'

'There you are, youngster,' he said to Tom, as he rejoined him, 'and mind you take proper care of your money in future.'

'Oh, Gore, you *are* a brick!' Tom exclaimed, his face brightening up as he grasped the money. 'However did you get it out of him?'

'Oh, I didn't have much trouble. He saw I meant business, and wasn't going to stand any nonsense.'

'And you'll promise,' said Tom, 'that you'll never say a word about it to any one?'

'Oh yes, I can easily promise that,' said Gore; 'for, now I come to think of it, we are both in the same boat; if you've been into the "Chequers," so have I.'

'Billy isn't likely to tell of us, I suppose?' said Tom, as the thought of that contingency crossed his mind.

'Oh no; he knows better than that, I expect.'

'I don't believe father would take his word if he did,' said Tom. 'Father thinks he's a thief, I know, and he used to tell awful lies when he was up at our place.'

'Well, then, we are safe enough,' replied Gore laughingly, 'so don't think any more about it.'

Meanwhile Webb and Emerton had been very differently employed. Striking straight across country for the distant Spinney, they had had a rattling run. The object of their expedition was to negotiate for some apples at a farmhouse situated near the Spinney. It was only occasionally that they attempted so long an excursion, but for some time past they had felt a yearning desire to taste again the luscious 'stubbards' with which Farmer Brown's orchard was so well stocked.

'It's blazing hot,' said Webb, as he made the best of his way along about two yards in the rear of Emerton. 'We shan't have time to eat many apples.'

'We can fill our pockets instead.'

In less than three-quarters of an hour they reached the edge of the Spinney, so that they had five minutes to spare before they need commence the return journey.

'Now, look out,' said Emerton. 'Here's the orchard. We must mind what we're about.'

'Are you going over?' asked Webb.

'Yes. We haven't time, after all, to go the farmhouse to get any milk.'

'Oh, I see,' said Webb, with a giggle. 'You aren't going to buy the apples this time?'

'Well, no,' said Emerton. 'We haven't time, for one thing, and if we had, I don't see the need of buying them; what difference can a dozen make to a man who's got an orchard like this?'

'All right! over you go,' said Webb. 'I'll keep cave this time—it's my turn.'

'Oh, bosh!' returned Emerton; 'let's both go; we shall get twice as many.'

'Well, I'm game,' agreed Webb.

A careful inspection showed that the coast was clear.

'Now then, fill your pockets as fast as you can,' cried Emerton, setting the example by jumping down into the orchard, and running to the nearest tree. In less than a minute they had crammed all the available receptacles about them with fine apples.

'I can't hold any more,' said Webb. 'We'd better make tracks.'

'All right. Up you get; I'll follow in half a second.'

Webb ran for an opening in the hedge and speedily climbed to the top; Emerton was over almost as soon, and they were on the point of leaping into the road when they heard a gig coming.

'Look out!' said Webb, jumping back into the orchard; 'somebody's coming.' Emerton was equally quick. They crouched down behind the hedge and heard the gig pass by. They were so intent upon keeping themselves out of sight of the road that they

THE EDGE OF THE SPINNEY.

61

had not noticed that the gate at the bottom of the orchard had opened and that Farmer Brown had entered it.

'Now then, over you go!' said Emerton. 'Look sharp!' At the same moment he turned to see that the coast was clear, and caught sight of the advancing farmer.

'Hi, you there!' shouted Mr. Brown; 'what are you doing in my orchard?'

Their only reply was to jump as quickly as possible into the road, and run at the top of their speed towards home. However, their progress was not so fast as before, for they were weighted by the awkward load they had to carry. Mr. Brown knew the bearings of the country better than they did, and, making no effort to follow them, ran across the orchard and through a field past which the road ran, thus cutting off a very large corner, arriving at the gate of the field just as the boys came in sight.

'Look out!' shouted Webb; 'there he is!' They stopped for a moment, and then began to run back in the opposite direction. The farmer, however, had sent a man round to follow them, so that they might be caught in a trap. The boys had not run many yards before they saw a labourer standing in the middle of the road evidently ready to receive them.

'By Jove! we're in for it now!' shouted Emerton. 'Come along!' He made a rush at the hedge on the opposite side of the road to that on which the orchard was situated, and, clambering to the top with some amount of damage to his hands and knees, stretched out his hand to help his companion over.

'He's close to us,' said Webb, in a frightened voice. Indeed the labourer was not more than thirty yards off.

'We're safe enough,' returned Emerton; 'he can't catch us up now.' A sudden thought struck him as he was leaping down from the top of the hedge into the field; he called out at the top of his voice, 'Come along, Gore!' Webb followed, and ran after him as fast as he could. Fear lent them wings, and in a few minutes they were safely out of reach of their pursuers. 'We're all right now,' said Emerton, panting. 'We shall get home in time, I think, after all.'

'I hope so,' Webb replied; he had thrown himself down at full length to recover his breath. 'But what on earth made you call out "Gore" for?'

'Did I?' asked Emerton innocently. 'I suppose it was in the excitement of the moment.'

'I suppose so,' said Webb. 'Shall we go on now?'

'If you're ready,' was the reply, 'I am.'

'Come along, then.'

As they reached the great gates, they heard the bell ringing for tea. 'Just in time,' said Emerton; 'that's lucky.'

CHAPTER VI.

GORE IN TROUBLE.

Next day, after afternoon school, Gore was somewhat surprised by a message from the Doctor that he wished to see him in his private room. John was the bearer of this message.

'Do you know what it is for?' Gore asked.

'No, Master Gore, I don't, but he's looking very black.'

'Hm! I wonder what it's about,' thought Gore. 'I

hope to goodness he hasn't heard anything about my going into the "Chequers" yesterday; I don't very well see how he could, though.'

It was with a very uneasy conscience that he found himself in the presence of the Doctor.

'I am very sorry, Gore,' began Dr. Russell, 'to have to make a very serious charge against you. Can you guess what it is?'

This was a question which Gore did not feel himself called upon to answer.

'I have received a letter,' continued the Doctor; 'it is from Mr. Brown. You know who he is, I suppose?'

'No, sir, I have never heard of him,' was the reply.

'He is a farmer,' resumed the Doctor, 'who lives near Hartwell Spinney. He writes to inform me that yesterday afternoon some boys robbed his orchard, and he has good reason for believing that they belonged to this school.'

The good reason for his belief was that the boys generally wore their cricketing caps when wandering about the village, and the cap was well known by the inhabitants around.

'What have you to say about it?' inquired the Doctor.

'Nothing at all, sir,' said Gore. 'I know nothing whatever of Mr. Brown, and I've never been near Hartwell Spinney in my life.'

The Doctor looked very angry. 'Be careful what you are saying, sir,' he said severely. 'Mr. Brown most distinctly states in his letter that the name of one of the robbers was Gore; his man and he himself both heard that name called out by one of the boys as he was clambering over the hedge.'

E

This statement took Gore completely by surprise.

'What have you to say?' again repeated the Doctor.

'Nothing but what I said before,' answered Gore; 'I was never near the place.'

The Doctor looked incredulous. 'Very well,' he said; 'of course if you were not there it will be very easy to prove it. Did you go out yesterday afternoon?'

'Yes, sir,' replied Gore.

'Where did you go?'

'Down in the village, sir.'

'Were you in the village the whole of the time?'

'No, sir; I was down on the beach part of the time.'

'Then of course some of the boys must have seen you if you were on the beach, for I know that several of them went down there. Whom did you see?'

'I didn't meet any one, sir; I went towards the Coast-guard, and I think the other boys went towards the bathing cove.'

'All this may be true, or it may be untrue,' continued the Doctor. 'As it at present stands, Mr. Brown distinctly states that you were at his orchard. You say you were on the beach, but can find no one who saw you there. The only way of clearing yourself will be for you to state in detail how you spent the whole of your time yesterday afternoon, between leaving the house and returning to it.'

This staggered Gore; it flashed across his mind in a moment that in order to do that he must confess his visit to the 'Chequers;' he remembered that he had given Tom a distinct promise that he would never say a word about that most unfortunate occurrence, and if he did confess it he knew that his situation would be by no means improved. In a moment his mind was made up.

'All I can tell you, sir, is that I did not go to the Spinney yesterday afternoon; that I have never been there in my life ; and that there must be some mistake on Mr. Brown's part.'

'Come, come,' said the Doctor rather angrily ; 'this is all beside the question. I asked you where you had been ; I don't want to know where you have *not* been.'

Gore did not make any reply.

'Where were you ?' again demanded the Doctor.

'I cannot tell you, sir.'

'But this is absurd !' broke out the Doctor. 'Do you expect me to believe that you were not at the Spinney, whilst you refuse to tell me where you were ?'

'I'm very sorry, sir,' said Gore, 'but it is the truth.'

'Oh, pooh, pooh !' rejoined the Doctor. 'Do you expect me to take your bare word for it against the distinct evidence of two men ?'

To this Gore had no reply to make. The Doctor rose from his seat and walked up and down the room.

'I must say, Gore, you surprise and grieve me very much. You have told me untruths.'

'I have not, sir,' broke in Gore.

'Don't interrupt me, sir,' said the Doctor. 'I have given you every opportunity of proving the truth of your assertions, and you have declined to take advantage of them. I have no alternative left me but to disbelieve you. If I were to do my duty I should refuse to let you remain longer at Eastcote, but that is a course that I am very loth to take. Go back to the schoolroom now, and this evening I will tell you what punishment I shall inflict on you for this dastardly conduct.'

Now that the Doctor had spoken, the main feeling in

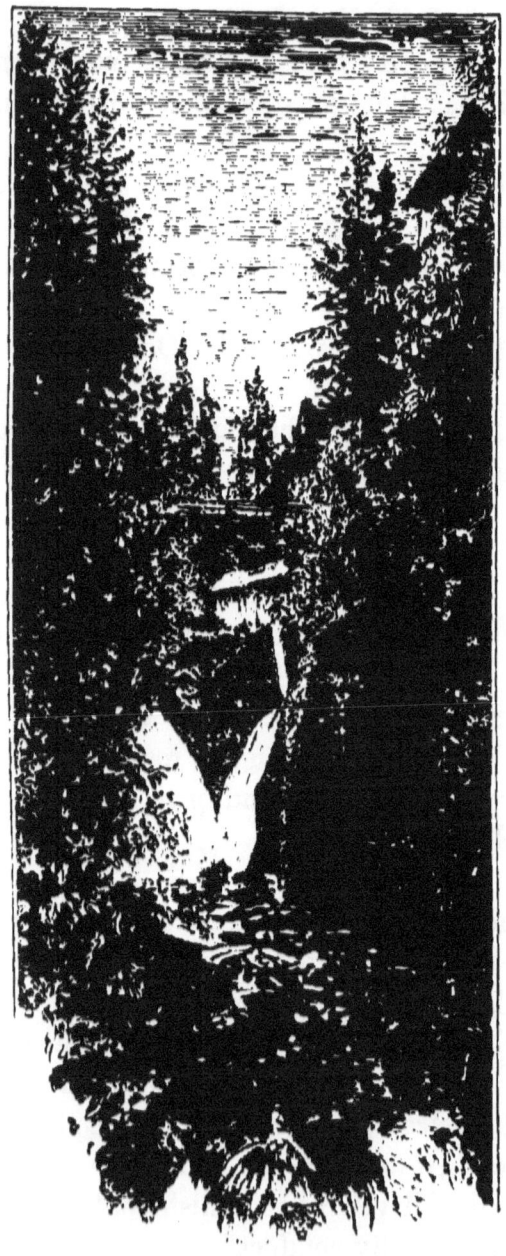

Gore's mind was one of resentment. It was intolerable that such an injustice should be done him. He did not mind what punishment might be given him — that was a mere trifle. The galling part of it was, that he had entirely lost the confidence of the Doctor, whilst he was quite innocent of the charge that had been made against him. It was an utter puzzle to him to think how his name could have been mixed up in the affair. He returned to the schoolroom, feeling more dejected and unhappy than he had been since he first entered the gates of Eastcote.

There was nothing for it but to wait with what amount of resignation he could till the evening, when he would know the punishment the Doctor intended to mete out to him.

After all, this did not prove to be so severe as he had feared. The Doctor informed him that he would be confined to the school premises for a week, and that he was to write out six hundred lines.

'Well, that's over,' thought Gore when he was in bed. 'It's not so bad after all. I must manage to do these lines without the fellows finding out that I've got into a row, or else they'll want to know what it is for. I wonder whether it was any of our fellows who stole those apples; if so, I must find him out, and if he won't confess it, I don't know whether I shan't confess it for him. I don't see why I should get into the Doctor's black books for the rest of my life here, when I have done nothing to deserve it.'

It struck him, as he lay thinking over the day's events, that he might have said that Tom was with him on the beach; but Tom's dread of his father was so great, that, were he to undergo a cross-examination, it would probably implicate both of them. Besides, Gore had no idea of the position of the Spinney, and, for all he knew, the fact that he was on the beach part of the time would by no means prove that he was not in the orchard previously.

Still puzzling his mind over it, he fell asleep.

'Single misfortunes never come alone,' says Sir Boyle Roche; 'and the greatest of all possible misfortunes is invariably succeeded by a still greater.'

Gore had quite set his mind on winning the scholar-ship at the approaching exam., and recently had felt that his chances of doing so were becoming brighter and brighter. But on the morning succeeding the inter-

view related in the last chapter, he found to his surprise
that when the Doctor took the first class in classics, in
spite of all his efforts he was easily distanced in his
translation of Horace by Emerton. At first he put it
down to the Doctor's unintentional preference for Emerton's
translation, having in view the fact that he (Gore) was in
disgrace; but he was soon obliged to acknowledge that
Emerton had made marvellous strides in construing since
the previous day.

'That is very good, Emerton,' said the Doctor, as
Emerton came safely through a very crabbed passage. 'I
was quite expecting that you would come to grief over
that irregular verb which Horace has used there in an
almost unique sense.'

'You take the next passage, Gore.'

Gore began his translation, but felt that he was not
doing as well as usual. During the previous evening's
preparation, his mind had been distracted by thinking
over the afternoon's events, and he was aware that he was
not doing himself, or his author, justice.

'That is not the gerund,' exclaimed the Doctor sharply,
as Gore went on with his translation. 'The slightest care
would have shown you that. What do you make of it,
Emerton?'

Emerton with the greatest of ease translated the passage,
and of course obtained precedence of Gore. This went on
during the whole lesson, as much to Gore's surprise as his
disgust.

When school was over, he took an opportunity of meeting Emerton, and strolled with him round the playground,
neglecting for the time those six hundred lines which were
hanging as a millstone round his neck.

' What's the row with you?' asked Emerton. 'It seems to me the Doctor was down upon you this morning.'

'Yes; I believe I've got into his black books,' returned Gore.

' What's that about?'

' Oh, never mind!' said Gore; 'some trifle or other. Something I said to him last night, I think.'

' It has put you off the mark, at any rate; at least I fancied you didn't do so well to-day as you generally do. I'd got quite resigned to seeing you ahead of me.'

' Well, it struck me that you were doing a great deal better than usual.'

'Yes,' rejoined Emerton. 'I've been too lazy up till now.'

'Have you ever been in to any exam. before?' asked Gore.

' Not many; the only one I ever did was the Junior Cambridge, at my last school.'

' We had a lot at the school I was at,' said Gore; 'I won two or three, but I got beaten once.'

' Oh!' said Emerton, in a nonchalant tone.

' Yes,' said Gore rather meaningly; 'but I got the prize all the same.'

'That was rum,' returned Emerton; 'how did it happen?'

' Well, we had a peculiar understanding at our school,' continued Gore. 'Fellows used to use cribs, you know; but then we had a clear understanding that, if a fellow used a crib, he was not to try and pull off a prize. He might use it to save himself from getting into a row for neglecting his work, so long as he did no harm to any one else; but if he used it when working up for any exam., that was quite another thing.'

' Oh!' said Emerton; 'that's a very good sort of understanding.'

' Yes, I think so too,' continued Gore. 'I found out

that this fellow who had beaten me had not only used a crib when working up, but had taken it into the exam., and had copied out some of his translations from it. I spoke to the monitors about it, and asked their advice, and they all agreed that that was a sort of thing that

could not be tolerated, so they sent for this chap and told him he'd better resign, and that if he didn't they'd take the matter into their hands and report him.'

'And did he resign?' inquired Emerton.

'Yes; he had nothing else to do.'

'Well,' was Emerton's next remark, 'all I can say is,

that if you let him use a crib all the time he was working up for the exam., it was rather a sneaking thing to do to report him for it afterwards.'

'It was a good deal more sneaking to try to win the prize by cheating, than to report the fellow afterwards for doing it.'

'That may be your opinion,' said Emerton, 'but it isn't mine.'

Gore had told this incident with a purpose. He had come to the distinct conclusion, from the way in which Emerton had done his translation that morning, that he had been using a 'crib.' He could not, of course, accuse him of possessing a 'crib,' because he did not know for certain that he had one; but he wanted a clear understanding with Emerton, that if he did use one, and it were discovered that he had done so, he (Gore) would have no scruple in exposing him.

'I suppose you've never used a crib?' queried Emerton.

'No,' was the reply. 'I don't think it's fair.'

'Some fellows are so confoundedly particular,' said Emerton, in a careless tone.

'Yes, and, on the other hand, some fellows aren't half particular enough,' retorted Gore.

'Do you mean that for me?' asked Emerton angrily.

'If the cap fits, wear it,' was the cool reply.

'Let me give you a word of advice: just mind your own business, and don't trouble yourself about anything else,' said Emerton.

'I'll take your advice,' said Gore, turning away. 'You'd better remember that I do mean to mind my own business, and that this exam. is distinctly my business.'

'Oh, go to ——,' exclaimed Emerton, walking off in the opposite direction without finishing his sentence.

CHAPTER VII

A VISIT TO THE SPINNEY.

GORE never found imprisonment so intolerable as during the succeeding week. He early determined that he would pay a visit to Mr. Brown at the Spinney, and try and clear up the mystery. But now he had his six hundred lines to write, and in addition to this he was anxious to give every spare moment to working up for his exam. He asked Mason at an early opportunity about the Spinney, and elicited from him that it was not an uncommon thing in the autumn for boys to make expeditions there when time allowed, and to purchase apples and milk at the farmhouse, but that as far as he, Mason, was aware, no one had been there during this term.

'I only wish I could go,' said Mason; 'but it takes such a tremendous time that except on half-holidays one

isn't able to get back before the bell rings, and on half
holidays they've always got some wretched match or other
on which you've got to play; but I'll try to go over with
you some day this week if you like. Suppose we go
on Thursday.'

'No, I can't go this week,' replied Gore, 'I've got so
much to do.'

'This blessed exam., I suppose?'

'Yes; partly,' answered Gore, not wishing to confess
that he had a punishment on hand.

But he found that he was not able to keep the fact of
his having lines to write so secret as he wished. Boys
have not that delicacy of feeling which grown-up people
possess, and Phillips did not think he was committing
any breach of ordinary manners in looking over
Gore's shoulder one day as he was busy writing out
his lines.

'Hallo, Gore!' he exclaimed; 'you don't mean to say
you're in for it?'

'Why not?' said Gore carelessly, as if it was the most
ordinary thing in the world for him to be writing moral
sentences.

'Why, what have you been up to?' inquired Phillips.
'I've never heard anything about it. Have you been
breaking bounds again?'

'No,' replied Gore; 'I didn't know that you'd heard
of that little joke.'

'Oh yes, I have, but what is it for?' he persisted.

'Oh, never you mind; you haven't got to write them
out, have you?'

'No, thank goodness! I've had about enough of
"Disorderly conduct meets with its due reward," and

"Deference to his superiors is the duty of every individual."'

Gore knew it was of no use to tell Phillips not to mention it to any one, so he continued writing without saying anything more ; and in a few minutes Phillips had informed half the school that Gore was in for some jolly row. Most of the boys were rather glad to find that the immaculate Gore was after all one of themselves, and perhaps Mason and Tom were the only two who were really sorry. Tom crept up to him as soon as he was alone, and in a frightened whisper asked him if it was about going into the 'Chequers.' 'Because, if so,' said Tom, 'it wasn't your fault at all, you know; it was all mine, and it isn't fair that you should get into a row for it.'

'Oh, nonsense !' replied Gore ; 'you needn't fret about that, my boy. It's nothing whatever to do with going into the " Chequers."'

'That's all right,' said Tom, his mind being relieved on that point ; 'but what is it for ?'

'Don't you bother about me,' said Gore. 'I shall knock this off by to-morrow ; and then next week we will go to Hartwell Spinney if you like. Mason's going with me, and we will get some apples.'

'Thanks,' said Tom, with effusion ; 'I'll come like a bird.'

Before long it came to Emerton's ears that Gore was in trouble. He had heard nothing at all about Mr. Brown's letter, and had concluded that the little episode was entirely over. It struck him now that there was a possibility that his ruse had succeeded, and that the blame which would otherwise have fallen upon his shoulders had fallen upon Gore's.

Meanwhile Emerton steadily continued ahead of Gore in classics. In spite of all his efforts Gore was unable to make certain that his opponent made use of a 'crib.' In mathematics he did not fear him; but at Eastcote, as at many schools, classics took precedence of every other study in the approaching exam. Strange to say, Gore did not at all connect the fact of Tom's visit to the 'Chequers' for the book with the fact that Emerton probably possessed a crib; Tom had never mentioned Emerton's name in connection with that visit, and consequently Gore thought nothing further about it.

Directly the week was over Gore went to the Doctor and asked permission to extend his next visit to the village by half an hour. The permission was granted, though not very graciously, for the Doctor could not forget that Gore had deceived him. Mason and Tom obtained similar permission, and the three boys set out on the Monday afternoon for Hartwell Spinney. The small boys led the way, for this was the first time that Gore had gone in that direction.

'Look here, you two,' he said, when they came in sight of the farm; 'here's a bob between you; go and get as many apples as you can for it, and have a good drink of milk. I want to speak to Mr. Brown whilst you are in there. I'll meet you round by the road in ten minutes.'

The youngsters raced off, knowing very well where to go to obtain the desired luxuries, whilst Gore made his way towards a barn, at the door of which he saw the farmer standing.

'You are Mr. Brown, aren't you?' he said.

'Yes, young gentleman, I am. What may you want with me?'

'You wrote to Dr. Russell the other day, complaining that some boys from our school had been robbing your orchard.'

'Yes, the young rascals, I did.'

'You said that the name of one of the boys was Gore. I am Gore, and I want to know why you thought that it was I who took part in it.'

'Why, because one of them called out your name,' replied Mr. Brown.

'Did you hear him call out?'

'Yes, and so did my man, Meadows, who was nearest to them.'

'Where's Meadows?' asked Gore; 'I should like to see him.'

'Oh, he's gone harvesting over at Farmer Fletcher's, and won't be back here for three weeks or more.'

This was a great nuisance; Gore did not know quite what was the next step to take.

'Look here,' continued Gore; 'you saw both of the boys who were in your orchard. Do you think that either of them was me?'

'Can't tell, I'm sure; one of them was about your height.'

'I suppose I must wait till Meadows comes back from harvesting,' he added.

'Oh, I shouldn't think anything more about it,' said the farmer. 'Here, come into the house and have a drink of milk, and you can go into the orchard and fill your pockets, for all I care.'

Gore did not decline his offer, and followed him into the dairy, where he found his two companions still regaling themselves, although they had had enough already to make it difficult to imagine where they were going to put the apples.

After spending a very enjoyable five minutes in the cool and airy room, they found it was time to be on the move again; in fact, they only had twenty-five minutes in which to make the journey home.

'Come,' said Gore, 'you'll have to put your best foot foremost; we shall have to run part of the way.'

'All right,' said Mason, who felt like a giant refreshed with wine; 'I'm ready.'

'Come along then,' said Gore, bidding good-bye to the farmer. 'You've got your apples?'

'Oh yes,' said Tom, with a grin.

It was easy to see that he spoke the truth, for every pocket was bulging out.

They went off at a smart trot down the road, but very soon the two youngsters gave in.

'Oh, I say,' said Mason, 'my wind's all gone. I can't run another step.'

'But you must,' said Gore, 'unless you want to be late.'

'I can't help it,' was the reply, as he sank in a heap on the ground. 'I feel as if I couldn't move another yard to save my life. I think I must have drunk a little too much milk.'

'I expect you have,' said Gore, with a laugh; 'how much did you take?'

'I only drank five glasses,' was the reply.

'I should think that's about enough,' answered Gore. 'But come along; I don't want to be late, after having asked special leave.'

By good fortune, at this moment a cart passed them, which was driven by one of Farmer Brown's men, who had seen them just before on the premises. He good-naturedly offered them a lift, and they were willing enough to accept it. The cart jolted fearfully, and both Tom and Mason felt uncommonly uncomfortable about the region of the stomach, Tom declaring that he felt sea-sick. However, they reached home without being actually ill after all, although their appetite for tea was considerably diminished.

The apples and milk must have got into Mason's head, for in the evening he had the effrontery to return a push which Emerton gave him for blocking his way in the passage to the lavatory. However, he took to his heels instantly, which might have been interpreted as an expression of regret for having forgotten himself.

'I'll lick you for that, you young sweep,' called out Emerton, not sorry to see that Gore was within hearing.

Mason shouted back a derisive reply, wondering how he could have the cheek to do it. He presumed, perhaps, on the fact that bullying had been much less frequent since Gore's arrival. Emerton had only exercised his tyranny when he was out of Gore's sight. But on this occasion he considered his honour was involved; he had said in Gore's presence that he would lick Mason, and it would not do now for him to back out of it on any pretence whatever.

'Come here, you little sweep!' he called out, as he saw Mason crossing the playground next day; 'I've got a word to say to you.'

Mason commenced to approach him, and then stopped. 'All right, what is it?'

'Come here, and I'll tell you.'

'Tell me from where you are. I can hear all you've got to say.'

Emerton's reply was to make a dash towards him, but Mason was on the look-out, and ran as hard as he could pelt towards the schoolroom. Gore was sitting there, working up his Greek. He looked up as Mason shot into the room.

'Hallo! is there a mad dog after you?' he asked.

F

'Pretty near as bad,' panted Mason, as he sank into a seat. At the same moment Emerton entered the room.

'Oh, there you are, you young rascal! I'll teach you to give me such a chase as this.' He went up to him and caught him by the arm.

'You let me alone,' shouted Mason. 'I've done nothing to you'—

'I'll let you go in a minute,' was the reply.

'Here, what's the row?' asked Gore.

'Emerton's going to lick me, because he pushed against me in the passage,' explained Mason, cowering down out of Emerton's reach as much as possible.

'You'd better let him alone, I think,' said Gore to Emerton.

'Oh! anything else?' was the reply. 'Are you going to be the protector of all the small boys in the school?'

'I don't know about *all* the small boys,' answered Gore, rising from his seat, 'but I am of this one at all events; he is my cousin.'

'Oh, I see!' returned Emerton; 'so, because he is your cousin, he is to be allowed to do just as he likes, I suppose.'

'No,' said Gore, 'but because he's my cousin *you* can't do what you like. Let him alone!' he added sharply.

Emerton dropped Mason's arm and walked over to Gore. 'You'll fight, I suppose?' he said.

Gore hesitated for a moment, then sat down in his place again. 'I supposed you were coming to that,' he answered. 'No, I don't want to fight.'

'Are you going to take a licking?' asked Emerton.

'Not exactly; but I'm not going to fight, I think we'd best leave that sort of thing to small boys; but, if you're

so very anxious about it, you can easily get your desire—
touch Mason again.'

Emerton grasped the situation, and determined to make
the best of it. ' You're a coward,' he said.

Gore rose from his seat once more, and Emerton began
to think he had gone a step too far.

' You'd better get out of this room,' said Gore.

' I'm not likely to want to stay in it with such a fellow
as you,' he retorted. ' I did think you had a morsel of
pluck in you, but I shan't make that mistake in future.
You're a confounded coward, and a disgrace to the
school.'

Two or three boys were in the room when this scene
took place, and they greatly wondered that Gore did not
accept Emerton's challenge; they thought that the latter
had the best of it. It was generally considered that when
one boy called another a coward, the latter had to prove
that he was not by fighting his accuser, but Gore had
taken the accusation with scarcely a word of protest. It
did not strike them Emerton was very careful to keep
clear of Gore's challenge in respect of touching his cousin;
all they remembered was that Emerton had insulted him,
and that he had swallowed the insult. Before the tea
bell rang, all the school was in possession of the fact that
Gore and Emerton had had a row, and before the evening
was over the school was split into two divisions, those
who sided with Gore, and those who took Emerton's
part.

Most of the boys were disappointed in Gore. They
had anticipated seeing him smash his opponent and their
old tyrant; now that he had not taken his opportunity,
but had rather seemed to shirk the encounter, they feared

lest they might come in for all the arrears of bullying which Emerton owed them.

The next afternoon was held the dancing-class. Gore, who belonged to it, felt it to be an awful nuisance to have to go, for he wanted every moment to work up for the exam., which would take place the next week. But

he was obliged to go, and his consolation was that Emerton would have to be there too.

By this time most of the fun had gone out of the class, and Tom, who had formerly looked forward to it with pleasure, found it on the whole a great bore; except for the fact that he met Florrie and Cissie there, he would have liked to have given it up. Mrs. Russell always brought the two young ladies, and, having seen them into the care of the professor, she generally went into the village to make calls, returning at the end of the lesson to take them back; so that Tom was able to have freer access to his sister than he generally could obtain. However, to-day his interview with her was interrupted by Mr. Wiggins exclaiming, in a harsher tone than he generally allowed himself to assume,—

'Don't lounge against the door like that, Mr. Emerton; it looks very bad indeed; no gentleman ever lounges about in that fashion.'

Emerton looked at the little professor rather superciliously, and said, 'I don't quite see how you can tell what a gentleman does.'

This of course was highly impertinent, and Mr. Wiggins felt it to be so; he coloured up as if he had been a boy. 'Mr. Emerton,' he stammered out, 'I'm surprised at you!'

'I daresay you are,' remarked Emerton coolly, 'but I can't help that.'

Gore thought it was time to interpose; the scene was becoming rather painful, for Mr. Wiggins was evidently growing very excited. 'At any rate, Emerton,' he said, walking slowly up to him, 'we are sent here to learn, so we ought to pay proper attention to whatever Mr. Wiggins may say.'

'I think so too,' put in Goodman, who took every safe opportunity of paying out his enemy.

'Do you indeed?' said Emerton sneeringly. 'Well, I suppose you two know as much of what a gentleman ought to do as Mr. Wiggins does.' Having said this, he took up his hat and left the room.

This appeared to be a challenge to authority, but it in reality was not so, for he had noticed that the time for the lesson was just up. A minute after, Mrs. Russell entered the room, and the class broke up without any further incident.

'I say, Gore,' remarked Goodman confidentially, as they walked towards the school, 'I think you ought to lick Emerton.'

'Do you want to see him licked?' inquired Gore.

'Yes, by Jove! I should think I do.'

'Then why don't you do your own dirty work?'

Goodman gave a sigh as he said sadly, 'I've tried.'

CHAPTER VIII.

A QUARREL AND ITS CONSEQUENCES.

WEBB found himself getting into trouble with more
frequency than was comfortable. He knew that he would
very soon be leaving school, and so felt more careless in
regard to its rules than he otherwise would have done;
but, unfortunately for his peace of mind, he found that
when he offended against the laws of Eastcote, the
authorities were as much down upon him as if they
anticipated his sojourn with them would be indefinitely
prolonged. The consequence was that day after day he
found himself burdened with impositions, and with very
little leisure time. This told on his temper, and he
became more irritable each day; this may account for
the following scene.

'Webb,' said Emerton, one day across the schoolroom, 'I want you to go down to town for me this
afternoon.'

'Then you'll have to want,' was the reply.

'I want a wax-end for my bat,' Emerton continued,
paying no notice to the interruption. 'You can get it at

the shoemaker's; it won't be more than twopence or three-pence at the outside.'

Webb did not reply at all this time.

'Do you hear?' cried Emerton.

'Oh yes, I hear fast enough, but I'm not going; I've told you so once.'

'Do you mean you've got some punishment?' asked Emerton.

'Yes, and if I hadn't I shouldn't go down to the village. I want to go to the Coastguard next time I go out.'

Emerton's reply to this was to seize him by the collar and pull him out of his place.

'You let me go, you brute!' shouted Webb; 'or I'll kick your shins for you.'

'You'd better not try, you little beggar.'

'I will. Will you let me go?'

But Emerton declined to accede to his request.

Webb kept his promise, and hit out wildly, at the same time kicking as hard as he could in the direction of the big boy's legs.

'I'll cure you of that,' said Emerton, and he commenced to give him a 'tanning.'

'All right, you beast!' sobbed Webb, crying with anger as well as pain. 'I'll pay you out for this.'

'Fire away,' responded Emerton; 'hadn't you better begin now?'

'Yes, so I will,' said Webb angrily. 'I'll tell the Doctor to-night about that crib.'

Fortunately for Emerton, no one else was in the school-room at this time; he glanced quickly round to assure himself of the fact, and then, walking over to Webb, sat down close to him.

'You young fool,' he exclaimed angrily, but still with considerable seriousness in his voice, 'you don't know what you're talking about!'

'Yes, I do,' blubbered Webb, 'and I mean it too. You touch me again, and I'll go straight in to the Doctor.'

'I'd smash you to jelly if I thought you would,' said Emerton; 'but you know better than that.'

'Do I?' was the response. 'You'll see.'

'Yes, you do. You can go in to the Doctor and tell him just what you like, but I shall have a word or two to say to him afterwards. Who got the crib sent? Why, you did, didn't you? and then lent it to me.'

'Yes, I remember,' replied Webb, seeing how he had been served in return, 'and I think you're the beastliest brute in the world.'

'Come, draw it mild; I'll make every allowance for your state of mind, but you mustn't use such words as that unless you want to get another licking.'

Webb muttered something unintelligible.

'Now then,' said Emerton, who saw he had completely regained his ascendency over the youngster, 'you can do just what you please, though I give you fair warning that if you don't keep your mouth shut you'll find that I shan't be content with simply licking you.'

'Why, what else can you do?' asked Webb.

'Never you mind! wait and see.' It was decidedly better to leave the threat vague, it would be more terrible.

Before the evening was out, Webb found many occasions to regret that he had quarrelled with his patron. It soon got about the school that Emerton had been licking him, and then Webb tasted all the bitterness of hoarded-up revenge on the part of those boys whom he had bullied in safety when Emerton backed him up.

However, Webb was not quite so stranded as he feared. It came natural to him to seek for a patron rather than a friend; in fact, there were but few of the boys of his own size in the school who would have cared to have chummed with him. By a curious series of events he found himself attached to Goodman. They had several strong bonds of sympathy; they both hated Emerton like poison, and were both afraid of him. Then, again, both of them were friendless, for Goodman had contrived to make himself thoroughly disliked before his fall, and even now was somewhat of a pariah. Webb was equally so, and thus the two boys found themselves thrown together a good deal, and formed a friendship of more sincerity than might have been expected.

'I'll tell you what, Goodie,' said Webb one day, 'when I am big, and come back from Harrow, I shall find out that fellow Emerton and give him a jolly good licking.'

'I hope you will,' replied Goodman.

'He's an awful sneak. He's going in for this exam., you know?'

'Yes,' said Goodman; 'but I don't think he'll win, will he?'

'Oh, won't he!' said Webb mysteriously.

'How?' inquired Goodman, fired with curiosity, and seeing that his companion was evidently concealing something from him.

'Why, he's got a crib!'

'Has he?' said Goodman, interested at once. 'Where on earth did he get that from?'

'I got it for him,' replied Webb, with a certain amount of pride in the fact; 'but I wish to goodness I hadn't now.'

They were seated in a corner of the playground when this conversation took place; no one was near them, and Webb seemed disposed to get quite confidential.

'You won't breathe a word of what I told you,' he said, 'if I let you know a secret?'

'No,' replied Goodman.

'Well, I can tell you where that fellow keeps his crib. It would serve him jolly well right, wouldn't it, if some one were to take it and hide it?'

'Yes, it would,' assented Goodman. 'Why don't you do it?'

'Oh, I can't,' replied the other. 'Don't you see that as I got it for him, and am the only one in the school that knows anything about it, if he were to lose it he would pitch on me directly. But look here, I'll tell you what we'll do; I'll tell you where it is, and you take it out and hide it somewhere, but don't tell me where, because he is sure to ask me if I've taken it, and I want to be able to say that I haven't, and that I don't know where it is.'

'All right,' said Goodman, 'I'll do it. I'll do it to-night,' he added decisively.

The next afternoon, taking his Euclid with him, Gore went out for a solitary walk along the beach, and found himself in the bathing cove. He lay down full length on the sand, and, opening his book, commenced a quiet hour's study; but in spite of himself he could not fix his mind on the propositions; his thoughts flew off from the circle ABC at a tangent, and he found himself ruminating over recent events. He was still thinking them over when they seemed to get mixed up with Q.E.D., and that with the ode '*Ad Mæcenatem.*'

Then he did not remember what he was thinking about, for, lulled by the murmuring sound of the rising tide, he fell fast asleep.

He woke suddenly with a sharp pain in his side; he jumped to his feet in a moment and looked round, but nothing was to be seen, yet he was quite sure that he had received a blow. It occurred to him in a moment that a small piece of rock must have become detached from the cliffs above his head and fallen on him; this explained everything, and without giving another thought to the matter he started for home. Just as he was about to turn the corner by the rocks, he chanced to look behind him and up the high cliffs. He there saw a figure climbing painfully and slowly up the perpendicular rock; he was within a few feet of the summit, and as Gore watched him gained the edge and disappeared. 'What on earth can he be up to?' thought Gore; 'he can't be bird-nesting this time of the year, and there is nothing else to go down the cliffs for. I wonder who it was.' It was impossible, however, to satisfy his curiosity, and as it was now nearly tea-time he again turned towards home, walking pretty quickly; but in spite of himself his mind ran continually on the scene he had witnessed; he kept wondering more and more what could have been the object of the climber. Even when he was in bed he could not shake his mind free of the subject, and it gained such a hold upon him that he inwardly determined at the earliest chance he would descend the cliff at the point where he had seen the man, and try to discover the meaning of his movements.

The next morning Gore prepared his lesson as carefully as possible, but by this time he had become quite reconciled to being below his rival when the classics came round. To his immense surprise he found on this occasion that Emerton was making fearful hash of his translation.

'What is the matter with you this morning?' inquired the Doctor; 'you don't seem to be doing as well as usual.'

'No, sir,' replied Emerton; 'I had a bad headache last night.'

'I am sorry to hear that,' said the Doctor. 'Do you feel unwell now?'

'No, sir,' said Emerton.

'You weren't able to prepare, of course?' continued the Doctor.

'No, sir,' was the reply.

'Then I will ask you a few questions on the preceding odes instead of going on with to-day's.'

This he proceeded to do, but became more and more annoyed as Emerton showed that his memory was completely at fault. Odes which a day or two before he had translated with perfect correctness, he now knew nothing of whatever. At last the Doctor ceased to question him, and turned to Gore, who acquitted himself fully as well as usual.

'That settles it,' said Gore to himself; 'he had a crib, but now he must have lost it, or else come to the end of it. There's a chance for me yet.'

Morning school was no sooner over than Emerton got hold of Webb and took him to a quiet spot in the playground. 'Now, you young beggar,' he said, 'it's no good your trying to fool me; where's that crib?'

' I haven't seen it,' said Webb sulkily.

' No bosh now ! No other fellow in the school knows that I've got one, and now I've lost it; you must have taken it.'

' No, I haven't,' returned Webb.

' I don't believe you.'

' I can't help it. I haven't seen the blessed thing.'

' Will you swear that?' demanded Emerton.

' Yes, I will.'

' That you haven't touched it?'

' That I haven't touched it, and haven't seen it, and haven't got the ghost of an idea where it is. It's no good your licking me ; I shan't say anything else, because it's true.'

' If it isn't true, I'll make you repent it to the last day of your life,' said Emerton.

Where on earth could it be? It was getting serious; if he could not discover it some time during the next day his chance in the exam. would be all over, for, trusting to his crib, he had never prepared a translation of any of the odes, and it was much too late for him to begin to plod through them now with the aid of a dictionary.

' I know who it is,' he suddenly exclaimed; 'it's that young Tom. He fetched the book up from the "Chequers," and he must have guessed what it was. Webb's put him up to it, I expect. What a young beggar it is !'

A few minutes more, and Tom found himself in the hands of his old tormentor.

' Have you seen a book of mine?' he inquired.

' No,' replied Tom.   ' Have you lost one?'

' Yes, a small thin book.'

' No, I haven't seen anything. What was the name of it ?' inquired Tom.

' It was like that one you brought up from the "Chequers," ' replied Emerton meaningly.

' Oh, was that your book ?' asked Tom innocently. ' I didn't know that. I thought it was for Webb; you told me it was, you remember.'

' Oh yes, so I did ; that was for Webb. It isn't that one I mean. You haven't seen it then ?' he added inconsequentially.

' No, I haven't,' replied Tom.

Emerton was afraid to make any further general inquiries round the school, as it would have aroused suspicion ; all he could do was to search in every nook and cranny that he could think of.

It seemed as if his chance of winning the exam. and the attendant £10 was gone like a flash.

Leaving the exam. to take care of itself, Gore obtained permission to go out that afternoon. His idea was to discover the meaning of the mysterious movement of the man on the cliff above the bathing cove. He found without difficulty the point at which the descent must have been made. There was a crevice between the rocks which made it possible to climb carefully on to a ledge some eight feet from the edge. The whole side of the cliff was honeycombed with holes in which numerous gulls built their nests. It seemed quite probable that the mysterious visitant had hidden something in one of these holes ; the question was, which opening had he selected ? Looking round to see that he was unobserved, he advanced to the edge, and step by step carefully let himself down the crevice. When he reached the ledge

he found that there were only three holes within his
reach; two of these were empty, the third he could not
look into, but could just reach with his hand. He leant
over, pushed his hand right into the aperture, and felt
that there was a book in his grasp.

'Why, what on earth's this?' he thought, as he drew
his hand out slowly, gradually working himself back to
the perpendicular. He managed to open it with one hand
as he held on with the other, and saw in an instant that
this book was Emerton's crib. 'By Jove!' he exclaimed;
'so he's been hiding it up here! No wonder that I never
was able to get a sight of it.' He put the book in his
pocket and then commenced to climb up the side of the
cliff again. To his discomfort, however, he saw approaching him in the distance none other than Emerton. He
clambered up the remainder of the cliff as rapidly as
possible, and managed to reach the top just as Emerton
appeared in view. He did not rise to his feet, but threw
himself full length along the path, as if he had lain down
to rest. Emerton came up to him in a few moments; at
first he appeared inclined to pass on without speaking,
but on second thoughts he stopped.

'What on earth are you doing here?' he asked.

'I'm resting,' replied Gore; 'I had a headache this
afternoon.' This was true enough, although it was
certainly misleading. 'By-the-by,' he continued, 'what
a hash you made of your Horace this morning! How
on earth was it?'

'I had a headache too,' returned Emerton; 'I suppose
you haven't a monopoly of them, have you?'

'Oh, by no means,' said Gore; 'but I hope mine won't
have such a deadly effect on my *memory*.'

'What do you mean?' cried Emerton, in a rage.

'Whatever you like,' was the reply. 'I warned you some time ago about that exam., and you didn't take my warning.'

'Well?' said Emerton.

'Well,' continued Gore, 'I mean to win that exam. if possible.'

'You confounded sneak!' burst out Emerton; 'you've been to my desk. That's what people call stealing.'

'Whatever are you talking about?' asked Gore innocently. 'I've never been to your desk in my life.'

Emerton looked at him doubtfully, as if he were inclined to disbelieve him, but even if he did he was not in much better case. He had the painful experience that his crib was gone, and that Gore knew that he had used one. What could he do? Apparently nothing. He turned on his heel and left Gore alone.

CHAPTER IX.

A STEP TOO FAR.

NEEDLESS to say Gore kept very careful guard over the 'crib' now that he had it in his possession. He felt now comparatively safe. Emerton had trusted so entirely to his crib that without its aid he must inevitably be stranded.

It may be wondered at that, when Webb instructed Goodman as to how he might obtain revenge on Emerton by stealing his crib, he did not destroy it in order to make himself safe in case of any possible discovery on the part of the authorities. The reason was that he had promised his brother faithfully to return it to him when done with. His idea was that it should remain hidden until the end of the term, when he could obtain possession of it and bid farewell and defiance at the same time to all the authorities at Eastcote.

The examination began. The boys worked their way

slowly through the long list of questions relating to intricacies of mathematics; they brought x to the nth power; they drew triangles on all sorts of lines, inscribed circles round various points; and altogether 'had a fine old time,' as Mason put it. Gore did fairly well, and Emerton, too, seemed pretty well satisfied with his work. In the afternoon came the classical exams.; here Gore seemed to have it all his own way. The ode chosen for translation chanced to be one which he knew specially well. Emerton's knowledge of it was decidedly superficial, still he did the best he could. He would have given a good deal to have won the exam., even if he never gained a penny by it, simply for the pleasure of beating his rival.

'I say, Goodie,' whispered Webb towards the close of the afternoon, 'Emerton doesn't seem to be getting on very much; he's struck; he hasn't written a word for the last five minutes. I've been watching him.'

'Serve him right,' said Goodman. 'I don't think he's much chance now.'

'Nor I,' returned Webb. 'Well, I think we've both of us taken our change out of him. What do you say?'

'Rather,' assented Goodman. 'I told him long ago I'd pay him out, and now I have.'

'I say,' continued Webb, in a whisper, 'I'm going to try to get to the Spinney this afternoon; will you come?'

'I don't know,' was the reply. 'It's a fearful long trot, and the chances are we shan't have time to get any apples when we get there.'

'Not if you go to the farmhouse,' said the youngster, 'but we needn't do that. All you've got to do is to hop over the hedge, and there you are—you can help yourself at your leisure.'

Goodman at length assented; they both had permission to go out that afternoon for the usual hour and a half, and on the day of examination it was improbable that discipline would be as strictly maintained as usual. There

was a sort of unusual sensation in the air, and boys neglected their lessons without coming in for their usual punishment. Every rule seemed to be more or less abrogated. However, rules were not so far relaxed as to enable the Doctor to overlook so grave an offence as coming in half an hour late for tea; and this was the offence which Goodman and Webb committed.

Webb had been continually in hot water of late; his offences had irritated the Doctor to a high degree. On the present occasion he sent for him, and, after reprimanding him severely, told him explicitly that the next grave offence of which he had to complain would result in his immediate expulsion. He received a heavy punishment,

and was confined to the school precincts for a week.
Goodman escaped rather more easily, as he had not
incurred the Doctor's displeasure recently.

The examination was over, and there was nothing now
to do but wait until the result was made known.

'Thank goodness it's over!' said Gore to his little
cousin, with a sigh of relief; 'I feel as if I had a big
weight off my chest.' He took a long yawn, and stretched
himself, evidently relieved.

'Exams. don't seem to agree with you,' said Mason.

'No, they don't,' was the reply ; 'and yet I've got to go
in for about a dozen, I believe, before I am a full-blown
doctor.'

'All medical ones?' inquired Mason. 'Can you describe
the circulation of the blood?'

'What on earth do you mean?' said Gore.

'Oh, that's a regular question to the medicals, don't
you know, and the answer is, "Down one leg and up the
other."'

Gore laughed, and, giving chase to the youngster, made
him spin round the playground at an unaccustomed rate.

'I say,' said Mason when he was caught, 'have you
heard about Webb?'

'No; what's the row?'

'He's in for a most awful shine. The Doctor's had
him up, and told him he'd expel him next time he came
before him.'

'What's that for?' asked Gore.

'Oh, nothing in particular—things in general. He's
been accumulating no end of atrocities recently, and
now matters have come to a crisis; there has been an
explosion.'

'It's his own fault,' said Gore; 'he's been a little fool, and he'll see it some day. I'm afraid that fellow Emerton hasn't done him any good.'

'I don't expect he has,' agreed Mason. 'Webb was quite a decent little chap when he came here first, before he got to be always about with Emerton. Thank heaven that that fellow didn't take a fancy to me!'

'Yes, you may well be thankful for that,' returned Gore seriously; 'it makes all the difference to a youngster when he first comes to a school whether he gets into a good or bad set. Mind you're careful, when you're grown up and become head boy, that you use your influence on the right side. You'll make many a fellow thankful for it in after years if you do.'

Mason promised he would, and Gore was satisfied that his little cousin, though somewhat mischievous, and decidedly thoughtless, had the making of a very decent fellow in him.

To return to Webb, who was fuming with anger at the Doctor's prohibition. He specially wanted to go down to the village next day, and, in fact, had arranged to go down with Goodman, and had obtained permission previous to his expedition to the Spinney. He thought it very unjust, and Goodman agreed with him, that that promise should now be revoked.

'Tell you what, Goodie,' he exclaimed, 'I'll chance it, if you will.'

'I don't much care about it,' was the reply; 'though, if we don't get that bat to-day, we shall have to give it up.'

'Yes,' said Webb ruefully, 'I've told Morgan I'd let him know at the latest to-day whether I would take it. It's a jolly good bat too; I wouldn't miss it for something.

Goodie, I'll go,—chance it all, — and you can come or not, just as you like, though, if you're half a fellow, you'll come.'

'All right,' returned Goodman, in desperation. 'I'll come. Why should I care?'

Both boys felt that the expedition was attended with considerable danger, but they laid their plans rather carefully. They arranged to go by different routes, and meet at a given spot. By good luck the Doctor went out for a walk directly after afternoon school was over; they watched him clear off the premises, and judged, by the direction he took, that there was no danger of his appearance in the village.

'I'm off,' said Webb. 'Don't you forget where we've got to meet.'

'All right,' said Goodman. 'I expect I shall be there first; you've got the longest way to go.'

'Never mind; I'll run,' returned Webb, and off he went.

Goodman slipped out and soon arrived at the main street of the village. Happening to look behind him as he entered it, he saw, about a hundred yards in the rear, none other than Dr. Russell, walking rapidly along. To dive down a by-street and stand in a doorway was the work of a second for Goodman; but, to his indescribable dismay, just as he left the main road he saw in the far distance Webb rapidly approaching. In three minutes at the outside he must meet the Doctor. Directly either turned the corner he must catch sight of the other.

'Oh, gemini! here's a go!' thought Goodman. 'What on earth can I do now? If I go out of here the Doctor will nab me as sure as life, and if I can't warn Webb he'll get caught to a dead certainty. Oh, thank goodness!' he ejaculated, as he saw some one approaching. It was Emerton.

Forgetful of the enmity which existed between them, Goodman jumped from his hiding-place, seized Emerton by the arm, and said imploringly,—

'Run as hard as you can and stop Webb. He's coming down the High Street, and the Doctor's coming down the other way, and they'll meet. He's out without leave.'

'Go and tell him yourself,' retorted Emerton, shaking his arm free.

'I can't,' said Goodman excitedly. 'Don't you know I'm out without leave too?'

A rapid thought shot through Emerton's brain.

'I'm not going to do your messages,' he said angrily.
'Don't you see that if the Doctor saw me with Webb I
should get into a row for telling him? You must look
after yourselves. If you choose to get into scrapes like
this you must find your own way out, that's all.'

He then walked on unconcernedly, and Goodman had
only just time to shrink back into his doorway as the
Doctor passed the end of the passage. Another moment,
as he well knew, and he must inevitably get sight of
Webb.

That was exactly what happened. Webb almost ran
into the Doctor's arms. He stopped short on seeing him,
hesitated for a moment, as if he would turn tail and run,
and then, seeing that flight would avail him nothing, he
stood and faced the Doctor. He did not see Emerton at
all, as he had kept carefully out of sight.

'What is this, Webb?' inquired the Doctor sternly,
surprised beyond measure to see him there. 'I thought
I told you not to leave the school for a week.'

'Yes, sir,' said Webb.

'Have you any excuse?' demanded the Doctor.

'No, sir,' was the response.

'Then come back with me.'

The Doctor took him by the arm and marched him
direct back to Eastcote. On arriving there, he took him
in by the front door of the house, instead of by the usual
entrance through the gates, marched him up-stairs, and
locked him into an unoccupied room.

In about half an hour the Doctor came back, opened
the door, and stood before the culprit.

'You know what I told you, Webb,' he said severely,
'and you know I am a man of my word. The house-

keeper has packed up your boxes, and you will leave
Eastcote by the first train to-morrow morning. I have
written to your father, who will receive the letter an hour
or two before you arrive.'

Poor Webb had nothing to say. He knew it was
hopeless to appeal to the Doctor's mercy, and he knew,
moreover, that he thoroughly deserved expulsion. However, now that the crisis had really come, the feeling of
desperation which had sustained him during the past

week entirely forsook him, and he began to cry most bitterly. The Doctor was touched, and, although he had no intention of altering his sentence, he laid his hand kindly on the boy's shoulder, and talked to him sympathizingly and earnestly, pointing out how his thoughtless and perverse conduct had entailed, not only trouble and pain on himself, but also on his parents, advising him strongly to turn over a new leaf, and at the school to which he might be sent on leaving Eastcote to try and lead a better sort of life. Webb promised he would. At all events, he now deeply regretted that he had been such a fool whilst at Eastcote.

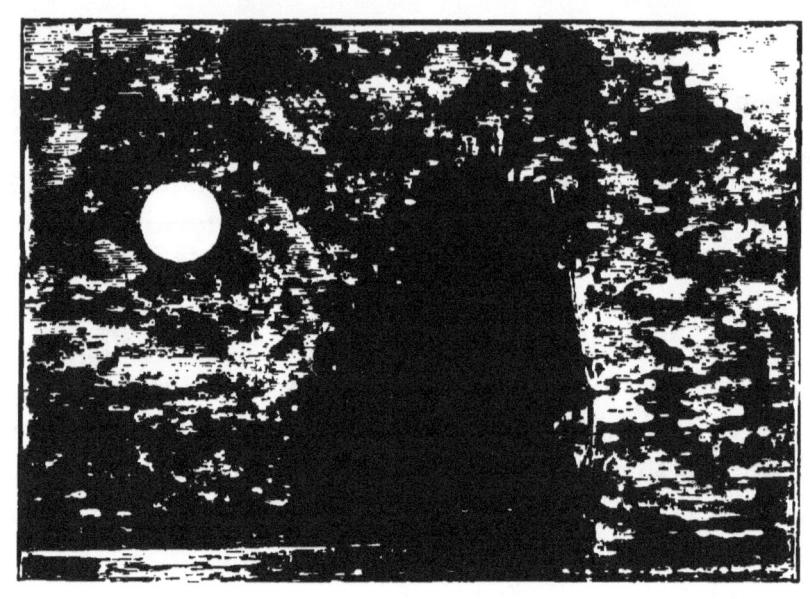

CHAPTER X.

HOIST WITH HIS OWN PETARD.

'I SAY, you fellows,' exclaimed Tom, bursting into the bedroom that evening, 'have you heard the news?'

'No; what is it?' asked Phillips sharply.

'Webb's expelled, and he's got to go away to-morrow morning.'

'By Jove!' exclaimed Phillips; 'it's come at last. I thought he would do for himself sooner or later.'

'But shan't we see him again?' inquired Goodman.

'No,' replied Tom. 'He's going to sleep in No. 17 to-night. His box is packed and all, and he's going by the early train to-morrow morning.'

'Well, I *am* sorry !' said Goodman. 'I don't know what anybody else is.'

Nobody else seemed to feel called upon to speak, and Emerton, when the news was brought to him, did not say anything, though he was secretly very glad to hear it. He would have had plenty of time to warn Webb of his impending danger in the village, but it had suddenly occurred to him then that Webb was the only boy in the school who knew that he had possessed a crib. Of course he was not aware that Gore had it. He thought that Gore had only surmised his possession of it. Webb, on the other hand, knew all the facts of the case, and could prove it. If Webb were expelled, he, Emerton, would be quite safe. No one could say that he had ever possessed a crib.

Goodman, who had formed a real liking for Webb, made an ineffectual attempt to see him before he left. Failing in this, he determined to write to him and tell him whose fault it was that he had been caught down in the village. He informed him how Emerton could have saved him from expulsion, and how he had refused to do so. This letter he persuaded a day-boy to post for him after morning school was over, so that Webb received it the day after he left Eastcote. Of course the despatch of this letter was entirely unknown to Emerton. He felt a weight had been removed from his mind when Webb had gone.

It happened that Gore and Emerton met in the play-ground after school, and Emerton took advantage of the opportunity to ask Gore, in a friendly tone, how he thought he had got on at the exam.

The two boys had not spoken to each other for the last two or three days, and Gore was somewhat surprised to find Emerton apparently wishing to be on good terms with him again.

'Oh, I got on pretty well, I think,' was the reply. 'How did you do?'

'Oh, better than I expected a good deal,' said Emerton, 'though I expect you pulled it off.'

'Well, I hope so,' responded Gore.

'How did you translate the bit "*Dulces docta modos*"?' Gore explained, 'Skilled in sweet measures.'

'But did you get that out of your own head?' inquired Emerton.

'No, I can't say I did. I got it out of a dictionary.'

'H'm!' rejoined Emerton; 'strange! I put that bit in, too.'

'Oh, did you? Did you get it out of a dictionary?'

'Never mind where I got it from,' returned Emerton, the fact being that it was a particular sentence he had chanced to remember from his crib.

At this moment something happened to interrupt their talk. Gore's answer had put a fresh idea into Emerton's mind; he had never been able to entirely satisfy himself on the point as to whether Gore knew more about the crib than he would care to confess, and Gore's reply about that particular passage seemed to confirm his suspicion that it was he who had obtained the crib; how or when he got it was a perfect mystery, because he fully believed Gore quite incapable of taking anything from another boy's desk. To go to another fellow's desk without his permission was a breach of school etiquette which was never committed; any boy who would dare to do such a thing would be speedily sent to Coventry by the whole school.

Two days afterwards, Emerton was somewhat sur-

prised at being sent for by the Doctor.

'What's up now?' he said to himself, as he went in. 'Is he going to tell me that I haven't won the exam., and wants to let me down easy?'

This, however, was not by any means the subject of the interview. The Doctor looked very grave as Emerton entered his private room.

'Emerton,' he began, 'I have received a most extra-ordinary letter, which, I am sorry to say, accuses you of the gravest breaches of school discipline. It is from a boy in whom I confess I can place but scant confidence, and I am unwilling to believe his assertions on his bare word; doubtless you will be able to disprove what he states.'

'I hope so, sir,' said Emerton; 'I am unaware of having done anything against rules.'

'It is from Webb,' continued Dr. Russell. 'He states that he and you, a few weeks back, robbed Farmer Brown's orchard at Hartwell Spinney. Now, you may not be aware that I have already severely punished one of the boys on suspicion of his having been concerned in this matter.'

'I was not aware of it, indeed,' answered Emerton; 'but I am bound to confess that Webb is partly correct in what he states. We certainly did go to the Spinney together, and he climbed over the hedge and stole some apples, although I had proposed to him that we should go round to the house, as usual, to buy some.'

The crisis had arrived, and Emerton was quite prepared, if necessary, to tell a direct lie in order to save himself.

'You know, sir,' he continued, 'that Webb and I were on very bad terms, and that he would be only too ready to get me into trouble if he could, without caring whether he spoke the truth or not.'

'No,' said the Doctor, 'I did not know that you had quarrelled; what was it about?'

'He wanted me to help him in his lessons, but I told him that I didn't think it was fair to the other boys, so I refused. He got very angry, and the result of it was, we quarrelled, and he said that he would pay me out some day, so I suppose the letter that you have received is by way of keeping his promise.'

'I hope I shall be able to look upon it in that light,' replied the Doctor; 'but he makes a still more serious charge against you. He says that he is certain that you possess a crib of Horace, and that you largely used it in preparing for the examination.' (Webb had, in his letter to the Doctor, carefully concealed the fact that he had obtained the crib himself for Emerton.)

'I am bound to confess,' resumed the Doctor, 'that I was rather surprised at the vast improvement which took place, rather suddenly, in your translations.'

'That was the result of my working harder than usual,' explained Emerton. 'I very much wanted to win this exam.; besides, the odes that I translated so much better than the others were a good deal easier.'

'That's partly true,' assented the Doctor; 'and I am bound to confess that in your examination you did not shine nearly so well as I had expected. If you had possessed a crib, I take it for granted that you would have made out a much better paper than that which you presented.'

'Do you mind telling me,' said Emerton, 'whether Gore or I did the best classical paper?'

'I did not intend to make the result of the examination known until to-morrow; but I may tell you that Gore has decidedly distinguished himself in classics, much to my surprise, I confess.'

'In that case, sir, which of us would you imagine possessed a crib?'

The Doctor looked utterly surprised. 'Why, you don't mean to say that you imagine Gore is capable of having used a crib?' he exclaimed sharply.

Emerton did not reply directly. 'I didn't accuse him, sir, of course; but I think that the great strides he has recently made in classics are at least as noticeable as those which roused your suspicion in respect of myself.'

The Doctor appeared to be extremely puzzled and

annoyed. It must be remembered, that although his confidence in Gore had received a rude shock in the matter of the robbing of the orchard, that was now explained; his reinstated confidence was now again shaken.

'There is an easy way of settling it, sir,' suggested Emerton; 'if you think that I possess a crib, I'm quite ready to have my desk searched, on the condition that Gore's is searched also.'

The Doctor hesitated. 'You are quite right, Emerton,' he said, after a little reflection; 'this is a very serious accusation to have made against any one. If you are both innocent, you will not object to proving it by having your desks searched; if you are guilty — But there, I will not contemplate such a possibility at present. Come with me.'

The Doctor turned to the schoolroom, which was now

completely deserted; he sent a message to Gore, saying that he wanted him.

'Gore,' began the Doctor, 'I have been informed by some one that a crib has been used by you or Emerton for this examination. The fairest way of deciding the question is to do as Emerton has suggested—to search both your desks.'

Gore coloured up in spite of himself.

'There is no need to search my desk, sir,' he said; 'there is a crib there, but it does not belong to me.'

'Give it me, sir,' said the Doctor sharply.

Gore put his hand into his desk and drew out the little book.

'Do you say this is not yours?'

'Yes, sir,' was Gore's answer.

'And do you, Emerton?'

'It is not mine, sir,' replied Emerton.

'Gore, come into my private room.'

Gore followed the Doctor, giving Emerton a glance of contempt as he passed, of which the latter took no notice.

'Now, Gore, tell me all about this,' said the Doctor severely.

Gore in reply gave him a history of all the events connected with the crib, describing how he had found it in the hole on the cliffs.

'How long have you had this?' inquired the Doctor.

'Ever since, sir.'

'That means several days before the examination?'

'Yes, sir.'

'I must say, Gore, yours is a very lame story. Whether you will be able to prove it to be true or not, you have laid yourself open to grave suspicion by keeping this book; you ought to have instantly brought it to me. Who was with you when you found it in that most unlikely hiding-place?'

'No one, sir,' Gore replied.

The Doctor frowned. 'It is a very strange thing, sir,' he said, 'that there never seem to be any witnesses when you are engaged in dubious actions. You have never yet

explained to me how you were occupied on that afternoon when Mr. Brown's apples were stolen.'

'I told you then, sir,' Gore broke out, 'that I had never been to Hartwell Spinney in my life, and you did not believe me; I cannot hope that you will believe me now, but it is the truth, nevertheless.'

'Circumstances have come to my knowledge,' replied Dr. Russell, 'which lead me to believe that you were not engaged in that robbery; but the punishment which you received for that offence was richly deserved by your refusing to inform me how you were employed that afternoon. Are you prepared to make any confession on that point now?'

'No, sir,' replied Gore firmly.

'Have you anything further to say with regard to your possession of this crib?' continued the Doctor, confirmed in his suspicion by Gore's refusal to explain matters in respect of the other point.

'No, sir,' again responded Gore.

'Very well, sir; I shall consider you as guilty. You will remain in exclusion from all the boys of the school, until I have had time to communicate with your parents. It depends on what your father may write to me, whether you will continue at Eastcote or not.'

CHAPTER XI.

THE LAST.

F course it soon became known through the school, how, none could guess, that Gore was in for a tremendous row. The curiosity and excitement on the subject increased every moment, and there seemed to be no means of allaying it. Poor Tom was in a most miserable state; ignorant of all that had happened, he feared that Gore's visit to the 'Chequers' had been in some mysterious way discovered, and that this row was the consequence. The poor little fellow could not sleep for thinking of it. He was passionately attached to Gore, and he fully determined in his own mind that, if this was the reason of Gore's disgrace, he would go straight to his father and confess the whole story; that at least would clear Gore. The difficulty was, how could he find out whether his suspicions were correct or not? He determined to try. He knew where Gore was confined; it was in a part of the house separated from all the other bedrooms. Tom

118

resolved to risk a visit to him. Slipping out of his bed about midnight, after all the other boys were asleep, he stole noiselessly along the corridor until he came to the door of Gore's room. He scratched on the panels gently at first, and then louder, till he heard a movement inside.

'It's only me, Gore,' he whispered through the key-hole.

'Who's me?' returned Gore, who, like Tom, had failed to get to sleep.

'Tom,' was the reply. 'Can you open the door?'

'Oh yes,' whispered Gore; 'it isn't locked.' He opened the door quietly, and Tom slid in.

'Well, what's the row, young un?' he asked.

'Oh, Gore, I couldn't sleep thinking about it,' was Tom's reply. 'I hear you're in for a most awful shine; is it about the "Chequers"?'

'Oh no,' said Gore, almost laughing in spite of himself at the way in which Tom's mind ran on that unhappy incident; 'it's about another thing altogether.'

'What is it?' asked Tom; 'do tell me.'

'Well, you may as well know,' said Gore; 'possibly you may be able to find out something for me which will clear matters up. It's precious cold standing about, though; come and tumble into bed with me, we will have a quiet talk; that is, if you aren't afraid of getting caught.'

'Oh no, I'm not afraid; none of the fellows are awake, and I can slip back at any time.'

So the two boys curled themselves up under the bed-clothes, and held a long whispered consultation. Gore told him the whole story, making him, however, promise not to spread it abroad unless he was able to discover some point which would make its disclosure advantageous. Tom listened very attentively, but could divine no way of proving Gore's innocence; in fact, it was very improbable that, when Gore himself could not demonstrate his innocence, a youngster like Tom should be able to.

'You d better be getting back now,' said the elder boy, when he had told him everything. 'Whatever happens to me, you, at any rate, will believe me innocent, and so will most of the other fellows, I think.'

'Yes, indeed,' said Tom, 'but I'm afraid that won't be much good. What a beast that Emerton is! I wish he'd never come near the school.'

'Oh, never mind about him,' answered Gore lightly; 'look on him as an awful example, and take warning by him. I'd sooner be in my place than his even now, by long chalks.'

'Oh, I say, Gore, you're a regular brick! I wish I was half like you,' said Tom warmly.

'Oh, nonsense!' answered Gore cheerily; 'I hope you'll be a good deal better than I am when you're as old as I. Now off you go, or you'll be catching cold.'

They wrung each other's hands warmly, not knowing whether they would have a chance of meeting again.

Tom crept back to his bed, and, now that his mind was relieved, soon fell asleep.

The next day was the dancing-class again. Gore of course was not allowed to go; he remained shut up in solitude in No. 17. Emerton also was conspicuous by his absence, for Mr. Wiggins had made a formal complaint to the Doctor with reference to his conduct at the last class, and the Doctor, after seeing Emerton about it, had decided that it would be on the whole better that he should not attend the remaining classes. Emerton had assured him that Mr. Wiggins had entirely misunderstood what he had said, and told him that he would be glad to be relieved of further attendance.

Goodman did not get on so well that afternoon as he usually did. He was in the habit of looking to Gore for hints as to the movements which he was to make, and in his absence he began to flounder about much in his former style. This roused Mr. Wiggins' displeasure, and, calling Goodman into the centre of the room, he put him through his paces alone. This gave Florence and Cissie the opportunity of asking Tom a question which had been on the tips of their tongues the whole of the afternoon.

'Where's Mr. Gore?' asked Florrie; 'he promised to dance with me this afternoon.'

'Ah yes,' said Rickards, coming up at the same moment; 'where is he, Tom? I hear he's in for an awful row; do you know anything about it?'

Tom decidedly did know, and was only too glad to unburden his mind on the subject. He rapidly gave them the history of the crib, and how Gore had discovered it in the hole in the cliff above the bathing cove. 'Father won't believe it,' he continued, 'and Gore can't prove it, because no one saw him there, and the puzzle is, who on earth could have hidden it there?'

'Yes, that's rather a poser,' said Rickards; 'I wonder who on earth it could have been.'

'I know!' said Florrie suddenly, in an excited whisper; 'I saw him do it.'

'Who?' exclaimed Tom and Rickards together.

'Him,' said Florence, regardless of grammar, pointing

with her finger to Goodman, who was floundering by
himself through the steps of the *chassez-croisez.*

'That fellow!' exclaimed Rickards.

'Yes,' answered Florrie; 'I'm sure of it. I was out for
a walk with Miss Fletcher' (Miss Fletcher was her
governess) 'when we saw him climbing up the cliff. I'm
sure it was he, but he didn't see us, he ran straight off
towards home.'

'By Jove, we've got it!' exclaimed Rickards excitedly. 'Don't say a word about it, Tom, till we get home—I'll come home with you.'

Tom could scarcely contain himself, but he managed to do so. Directly the class was over, he and Rickards rushed out and waited for Goodman.

'I say, Goodman,' said Rickards, taking his arm and marching him along, 'we've got something to talk to you about.'

'What's the row?' inquired Goodman.

Rickards, without giving Tom a chance to put a word in edgeways, sideways, or any other way, told Goodman the history of Gore's disgrace. 'We know all about it, you see,' he continued. 'Now you'll have to go and tell the Doctor the whole story; we aren't going to let Gore get expelled for nothing.'

'Oh, I say,' said Goodman, 'but I shall get into a jolly row too!'

'Why, you selfish beggar,' broke out Rickards, 'are you going to let a good fellow be expelled in order to save yourself from getting into a row? I tell you what,—if you don't go and tell the Doctor at once, I will.'

'I didn't say I wasn't going to tell him!' returned Goodman sulkily. 'After all,' he said, brightening up, 'I don't suppose I shall get into such a row as that Emerton, —it was all his fault.'

'I don't care who gets into a row,' chimed in Tom, 'so long as Gore gets out of it.'

'In you go now; don't lose time,' urged Rickards.

They arrived at the school gates. Rickards never let go of Goodman's arm, but marched him straight into the house, and knocked at the Doctor's private door, asking if they might speak to him just a moment.

'Yes,' was the reply.   'What is the matter?'

Tom and Rickards both began to explain together, and got so mixed up in their excitement, that the Doctor soon had to call upon Tom to continue alone.   This he did in an eager and broken manner, making, however, his meaning sufficiently plain to his father.

'So, Goodman,' said the Doctor, when Tom had finished, 'you were the one to hide the book?'

'Yes, sir,' replied he; 'I took it out of Emerton's desk, to pay him out.'

'To pay him out for what?'

'He licked me, sir, at the beginning of the term,' was the answer.

'Oh! so you fought, did you?' the Doctor asked.

'Yes, sir,' said Goodman, almost regretting that he had confessed it.

'I shall have a word to say to you about that by-and-by,' said the Doctor.   He rang a bell, and sent a message for Emerton to appear before him.

'Emerton,' said Dr. Russell very sternly, when he came into the room, 'I have received some information which now puts matters in a very different light.   I may tell you it will be better for you to make a full confession of everything.'

Emerton stood for a moment hesitating; he saw from the Doctor's look that the game was up.   His only hope was that he did not know quite so much as he pretended; he knew that, if he did confess, expulsion would be the inevitable result, so he determined to risk his last chance of escape.

'I have nothing to confess, sir, beyond what I told you this morning.'

'Is that all you have to say?' inquired the Doctor slowly.

'Yes, sir,' Emerton replied.

'Very well,' said the Doctor. 'You can now return to the schoolroom,' he said to the other three boys; 'you, Emerton, remain here.'

.   .   .   .   .   .

There is not much more to tell. As Emerton had anticipated, he was expelled. Before he left, he heard the full story of the discovery, and one of his chief regrets in leaving was, that he had no opportunity of paying out Goodman for his tardy revenge on him.

Needless to state, Gore was speedily sent for and liberated; the Doctor's confidence in him was perfectly restored, and he assured Gore that he was quite ready to believe that he had never opened the crib from the moment when it came into his possession. Whether Emerton had been expelled or not, the result of the examination would have been the same, for Gore's papers were, in almost every case, superior to those of his rival.

Tom and Mason had 'a tall time of it' next day, for Gore, in his gladness of heart at the joyous change in his circumstances, took them down to the village and gave them *carte blanche* at the 'tuck' shop, a privilege of which they both availed themselves to an alarming extent.

The Doctor wrote to Gore's father by the first post, after he had discovered the real state of affairs, unreservedly withdrawing all charges against his son, and stating that in every respect he was more than satisfied with his conduct, and would be proud for him to remain at East-cote, until it was necessary for him to leave for college.

After Emerton's departure the school seemed to take a new lease of life. Goodman never attempted to make a rival of Gore : for one thing, it would have been useless to attempt it ; and for another, he had a great admiration of him—an admiration which Gore was able to turn to good use by striving to make a better fellow of him.

When at the end of the year the school broke up, and Gore left Eastcote for college, there was not a boy who did not regret his departure,—not one who did not hope that, at his own farewell to Eastcote, the regrets of his companions might be half as genuine and sincere.